"Do you believe in destiny, Nick? Do you believe in fate?"

"Only as a last resort. Why?"

"I think we should let the game decide. Xia and Shang against the Martians. If we win we go to Hong Kong as man and wife. If we lose, you throw yourself on the tender mercies of Mr. Tey and spill your guts."

"You're serious, aren't you?"

She was.

"Deal," he said, and the fighting began.

Two murderous hours later it was decided. They were going to Hong Kong.

THE ELIGIBLE BACHELORS

They're strong, sexy, seductive...
and single!

These gorgeous men are used to driving women wild—they've got the looks, the cash and that extra special something....

They're also resolutely commitment-free! But will these bachelors change their playboy ways after meeting our four feisty females?

Find out in this month's collection from Promotional Presents!

Available now:

Wife for a Week
Kelly Hunter

Mistress on Trial
Kate Hardy

MacAllister's Baby
Julie Cohen

The Firefighter's Chosen Bride
Trish Wylie

WIFE FOR A WEEK

KELLY HUNTER

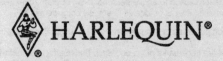

TORONTO • NEW YORK • LONDON
AMSTERDAM • PARIS • SYDNEY • HAMBURG
STOCKHOLM • ATHENS • TOKYO • MILAN • MADRID
PRAGUE • WARSAW • BUDAPEST • AUCKLAND

ISBN-13: 978-0-373-82053-5
ISBN-10:   0-373-82053-4

WIFE FOR A WEEK

First North American Publication 2007.

Copyright © 2006 by Kelly Hunter.

This edition published by arrangement with Harlequin Books S.A.

® and TM are trademarks of the publisher. Trademarks indicated with
® are registered in the United States Patent and Trademark Office, the
Canadian Trade Marks Office and in other countries.

www.eHarlequin.com

Printed in U.S.A.

WIFE FOR
A WEEK

To generous hearts

CHAPTER ONE

HALLIE BENNETT had been selling shoes for exactly one month. One long, mind-numbing month working solo at the exclusive little shoe shop in London's fashionable Chelsea, and she really didn't think she'd last another. Back in the storeroom she'd sorted every pair of shoes by designer, then model and finally by size. Out here on the shop floor she'd arranged the stock by colour and within the colours, by function. Dusting and vacuuming? Done. Serving customers? Not yet but, hey, it was only midday.

Hallie picked up the nearest shoe, a pretty leopard-print open-toed sandal with an onyx heel, and tried to figure out why anyone would actually pay three hundred and seventy-five pounds for a pair of them. She dangled it from her fingertips, turned it this way and that before finally balancing it on her palm.

'So what do you think, shoe? Are we going to cram a sweet size six like you onto a size eight foot today?'

A quick jiggle made the shoe nod.

'I think so too but what can I do? They never listen. These women wouldn't be caught dead in a size eight shoe. Now if they were men it'd be different. As far as men are concerned, the bigger the better.' The door to the shop opened, the bell tinkled, and Hallie hurriedly set the shoe back on its pedestal and turned around.

'Darling, what a thoroughly daunting shop! I swear, until I saw you talking to that shoe I didn't dare come in.'

The woman who had spoken was a study in contradictions. Her clothes were pure glamour, and her figure was a triumph over nature considering that she had to be in her late fifties. But her wrinkles were unironed, her hair was grey, and her 'darling' had been warm, possibly even genuine.

'Come on in,' said Hallie with a smile. 'Look around. Trust me, they never talk back.'

'Oh, you're an Australian!' said the woman, clearly delighted with the notion. 'I love Australian accents. Such marvellous vowel sounds.'

Hallie's smile widened, and she spared a glance for the woman's companion as he followed her into the shop, a glance that automatically upgraded to a stare because, frankly, she couldn't help it.

As far as women's fashion accessories went, he was spectacular. A black-haired, cobalt-eyed, dangerous-looking toy who no doubt warned you outright not to bother playing with him if you didn't like his rules. He was like a Hermès handbag; women saw and women wanted, even though they knew the price was going to be astronomical. And then he spoke.

'She needs a pair of shoes,' he said in a deep baritone that was utterly sexy. 'Something more appropriate for a woman her age.'

'You're new at this, aren't you?' muttered Hallie before turning to stare down at the woman's shoes, a stylish pair of Ferragamo man-eaters with a four-inch heel. They were a perfect fit for the woman's perfectly manicured size-six feet. They were fire-engine red. 'There is *nothing* wrong with those shoes,' said Hallie reverently. 'Those shoes are gorgeous!'

'Thank you, dear,' said the woman. 'Why a woman turns fifty and all of a sudden certain people to whom she gave birth start thinking she should be wearing orthopaedic shoes is completely beyond me.' The woman seemed to age ten years as wrinkles creased and unshed tears leached even more colour from eyes that would have once been a bright sparkling blue. 'Your father would have loved these shoes!'

Ah. It was all starting to make sense. He of the indigo glare was the woman's son and right now he was in big trouble. 'Right,' said Hallie brightly. 'Well, I'll just be over by the counter if you need me.'

He moved fast, blocking her escape. 'Don't even think of leaving me alone with this woman. Give her some shoes to try on. Anything!' He picked up the open-toed leopard-print sandal. 'These!'

'An excellent choice,' she said, deftly plucking it from his hand. 'And a steal at only three hundred and seventy-five pounds. Maybe your mother would like two pairs?'

His eyes narrowed. Hallie smiled back.

'If only I had something to look forward to,' said the woman with a sigh that was pure theatre as she sat on the black leather sofa and slipped off her shoes. 'Grandchildren, for instance. I need grandchildren.'

'Everyone needs something,' said her son, looking not at his mother but at her. 'What do *you* need?'

'Another job,' said Hallie, kneeling to fit the sandals. 'This one's driving me nuts.' She sat back on her heels and surveyed the sandals. 'They fit you beautifully.'

'They do, don't they?'

'How do you feel about travel?' he asked her while his mother preened.

'Travel is my middle name.'

'And your first name?'

'Hallie. Hallie Bennett.'

'Nicholas Cooper,' he said and gestured towards the woman. 'My mother, Clea.'

'Pleased to meet you,' said Clea, her handshake warm and surprisingly firm. 'Nicky, she's darling! She's perfect! You need a wife; you said so this morning. I think we've just found her.'

'Wife?' said Hallie. *Wife?* That'd teach her to shake hands with strangers. Nicholas Cooper's smile was lazy. His mother's was hopeful. Probably they were both mad.

'He's loaded,' said Clea encouragingly.

'Well, yes.' She could see that from the way he dressed. He was also far too amused for his own good. 'But is he creative?'

'You should see his tax return.'

'I don't know, Clea. I think I prefer my men a little less…' What? She slid Nicholas Cooper another quick glance. Sexy? Wild? Gorgeous? 'Dark,' she came up with finally. 'I prefer blonds.'

'Well, he's not a blond,' conceded Clea, 'but look at his feet.'

Everyone looked.

He wore hand-stitched Italian leather lace-ups. Size twelve. Wide.

'Of course, as his mother I can't let you marry him unless you're compatible, so maybe you should just kiss him and find out.'

'What? Now? Ah, Clea, I really don't think—'

'Don't argue with your future mother-in-law, dear. It's bad form.'

'No, really, I can't. It's not that, er, *Nicky* doesn't have a lot going for him—'

'Thanks,' he said dryly. 'You can call me Nick.'

'Because clearly he does. It's just that, well…' She cast about for a reason to resist. Any reason. Yes, that would do. It wasn't quite the truth, but little white lies were allowed in sticky situations, right? 'I wouldn't be very good wife material right now. I have a broken heart.'

'Oh, Hallie, I'm so sorry,' said Clea in a hushed voice. 'What happened?'

'It was terrible,' she murmured. 'I try not to think of it.'

Clea waited expectantly.

Obviously she was going to have to think of something. Hallie leaned forward and tried to look suitably woebegone. 'He was secretly in love with his football coach the whole time we were together!'

'The cad!' said Clea.

'Was he blond?' said Nick. 'I'm betting he was blond.' He was standing beside her, close, very close, and she was kneeling there, her gaze directly level with…oh!

'Are you *sure* you're not interested?' asked Clea.

Hallie nodded vigorously and dropped her gaze, looking for carpet and finding feet. Big feet. 'It's this job,' she muttered, more to herself than anyone else. Probably he was bluffing. Probably he had regular size-eight feet tucked into those enormous shoes. Her hand shot out of its own accord, spanning the soft leather of his shoe, testing the fit for width and finding it tight. Right. She pressed her thumb down and felt for toes, found them at the very top of the shoe. 'Phew!' She felt breathless. 'It's a tight fit.'

'Always,' he said, amusement dancing in his eyes. 'But I'm used to it.'

Hallie smiled weakly and scrambled to her feet as warmth spread rapidly through her cheeks. It was his eyes. His voice. Possibly his feet. Any one of them was a guaranteed temptation, but all three together? No wonder she was blushing.

'What my mother meant to say was that I need someone to *pretend* to be my wife for a week. Next week to be precise. In Hong Kong. You'd be reimbursed of course. Say, five thousand the week, all expenses covered?'

'Five thousand pounds? For a week's work?' There had to be a catch. 'And what exactly would I have to do to earn that five thousand pounds?'

'Share a room with me, but not a bed, which is fortunate considering your broken heart.'

Was he laughing at her? 'What else would I have to do?'

'Socialize with my clients; act like my wife.'

'Could you be a little more specific?'

'Nope. Just do whatever it is wives do. I've never had one; I wouldn't know.'

'I've never been one. I wouldn't know either.'

'Perfect,' said Clea, bright-eyed. 'I'm believing it already. Of course if the kiss isn't convincing it's just not going to work.'

'No kissing,' said Hallie. 'I'm heartbroken, remember?'

'There has to be kissing,' he countered. 'It's part of the job description. Who knows? You might even like it.' There was a subtle challenge to his words, lots of amusement.

'Kissing would cost extra,' she informed him loftily. What did she have to lose? It wasn't exactly the sanest of conversations to begin with.

'How much extra?'

Hallie paused. She needed ten thousand pounds to finish her Sotheby's diploma in East Asian Art; she had five of it saved. 'I'm thinking another five thousand should do it.'

'Five thousand pounds for a few kisses?' He sounded incredulous, still looked amused.

'I'm a very good kisser.'

'I think I'm going to need a demonstration.'

Now she'd done it. She was going to have to kiss him. Fortunately common sense kicked in and demanded she make it brief. And not too enthusiastic. One step put her within touching distance; a tilt of her head put her within kissing range. She stood on tiptoe and set her hands to his chest, found his shirt soft and warm from the wearing, with a hard wall of muscle beneath. But she digressed. With a quick breath, Hallie leaned forward and set her mouth to his.

His lips were warm and pleasant; his taste was one she could get used to. She didn't linger.

'Well, that was downright perfunctory,' he said as she pulled away.

'Best I can do given the circumstances.' Hallie's smile was smug; she couldn't help it. 'Sorry. No spark.'

'I'm not sure I can justify paying five thousand pounds for kisses without spark.' His lips twitched. 'I'm thinking spark is a must.'

'Spark is not part of the negotiation,' she said sweetly. 'Spark is a freebie. It's either there or it's not.'

'Ah.' There was a gleam in his eyes she didn't entirely trust. 'Turn around, Mother.' And without waiting to see if his mother complied, Nicholas Cooper threaded his hands through her hair and his mouth descended on hers.

Hallie didn't have time to protest. To prepare herself for his invasion as he teased her lips apart for a kiss that was anything but perfunctory. Plenty of chemistry here now, she thought hazily as his lips moved on hers, warm, lazy, and very, very knowledgeable. Plenty of heat as her mouth opened beneath his and she tasted passion and it was richer, riper than she'd ever known. She melted against him, sliding her hands across his shoulders to twine around his neck as he slanted his head and took her deeper, tasting her with his tongue, curling it around her own in a delicate duel.

If this was kissing, she thought with an incoherent little gasp, then she'd never really been kissed before.

If this was kissing, imagine what his lovemaking would be like.

His smile was crookedly endearing when he finally lifted his mouth from hers, his hands gentle as he smoothed her hair back in place. 'Now that was much better,' he said in that delicious bedroom voice, and she damn near melted in a puddle at his size-twelve feet. 'We'll take the shoes.'

Right. The shoes. She boxed the sandals with unsteady hands, swiped his credit card through the machine, fumbled for a pen and waited for him to sign the docket before she risked looking at him again. His hands were large like his feet, and his hair was mussed from where *her* hands had been.

What would it be like to pretend to be this man's wife for a week? Foolish, certainly, not to mention hazardous to her perfectly healthy sex drive. What if he *was* as good as his kiss implied? What if they did end up doing…it? Who would ever measure up to him again?

No. Too risky. Besides, she'd have to be crazy to go to Hong Kong for a week with a perfect stranger. What if he was a white-slave trader? What if he left her there?

What if he was perfect?

He was halfway across the room before she opened her mouth. Almost to the door before she spoke. 'So you'll get back to me on the wife thing?'

At five thirty-five that afternoon, Hallie counted the day's take. It wasn't hard; she'd only made three sales and that included the shoes Nicholas Cooper had purchased for his mother. Next, she shut the customer door, turned the elegant little door sign to 'closed', and was about to set the alarm system when a breathless courier rapped on the display window and held up a flat rectangular parcel.

Not shoes, thought Hallie. Shoes did not arrive by courier in flat little parcels, even designer ones. But the courier's credentials looked real, the address on the parcel was that of the shop, and the name on the paperwork was hers so she opened up with a sigh, signed for the parcel, and locked up behind him before turning back to the parcel.

It was a brown-paper package tied up with string. Hallie snipped and ripped to reveal a slim travel guide to Hong Kong and Nicholas Cooper's business card. The card said he was a software developer. Good to know. She flipped it over and discovered a message on the back.

'Marco's on Kings,' it read in bold black scrawl, and beneath that, '7 p.m. tonight, Nick.'

Presumptuous, yes, he was certainly that. His kiss had been presumptuous too.

Not to mention annoyingly unforgettable.

So what if Marco's was one of the best seafood restaurants this side of heaven? No sensible woman would even consider his proposal. Pretending to be a complete stranger's wife for a week was ridiculous, even by her standards.

And yet...

Hallie reached for the travel guide and smoothed it open, first one page, and then another.

Hong Kong: gateway to the orient. Money and superstition. Heat and a million camera shops. A squillion neon signs.

'An enchanting blend of East meets West,' read the travel guide. Half a world away from this shoe shop, whispered her brain. Ten thousand pounds.

So there were a few drawbacks.

Lies. Deception. Nick Cooper's kisses. Hallie tucked a stray strand of hair behind her ear and closed the book with a snap.

Big drawbacks.

And yet...

Twenty minutes later, Hallie let herself in through the front door of her brother's Chelsea flat and dumped her handbag on the sideboard. Why Tris had bought the little two-bedroom apartment when he never stayed more than a year in any one place was a mystery, but she certainly appreciated the use of it. She'd never save enough money to finish her diploma if she had to pay rent. Not on her current wage, at any rate.

Ten thousand pounds, whispered her brain as she slipped off her shoes and padded down the hallway.

No.

Dinner at Marco's, then. It's only dinner.

No, it's not. If you go to dinner you'll ask him why he needs a wife for a week and then where will you be? Next thing you know, you'll be agreeing to go to Hong Kong with him.

So?

Oh, boy. Hallie stumbled over the hallway runner and wondered just what it was about Nicholas Cooper that made her lose her mind.

He had a wicked smile. No doubt about it.

And his offer was definitely intriguing.

A rueful smile tugged at her lips. Best not to even think about his kisses.

Come ten to seven, Hallie had finished her argument and was in the bathroom, hurriedly applying make-up, when she heard the front door open and close, followed by the sound of a man's long, loping strides down the hall. Moments later Tris appeared in the doorway, little more than a vague shadow at the edge of her vision. 'You're back,' she said, busy with the mascara. 'I wasn't expecting you until tomorrow.'

'Plans change,' he said. 'Going somewhere?'

'Dinner at Marco's on Kings Road.'

'Classy.' Was it just her imagination or was Tris a whole lot more preoccupied than usual. 'Who with?'

Ah. That was more like it. 'Nick.'

'Nick?'

'We met today. At the shop.'

'He wears ladies' shoes? Is this supposed to be reassuring?'

'He came in with his mother. He *bought* her some shoes.'

'Run,' said Tris. 'Run the other way.'

'Nope. I've made up my mind. I'm having dinner with him.' She finished with the mascara, reached for a smoky grey eyeliner.

'So…' said Tris. 'Does *Nick* have a last name?'

'Of course he does, but if I tell it to you you'll run a check on him at work and come home and tell me what kind of toothpaste he uses. Where's the fun in that? Besides, it's not even a date, exactly. More of a business opportunity.'

'What kind of business opportunity?'

'I'm not sure yet.' No need to bore him with details. 'Something involving travel.'

Tris sighed, heavily. 'And you believed him.'

Time to change the subject. 'There's leftover lasagne in the fridge,' she said as she dropped her lipstick into her evening bag and turned to leave the bathroom, halting abruptly as she took her first good look at her brother. 'Whoa.' His dark, shaggy hair was filthy, his left hand was carelessly bandaged and his clothes looked as if they'd been dragged through a sewer with him still wearing them, but it was his eyes that bothered her most. Because they were full of frustration and pain. 'You look terrible.'

'I'm fine.'

'Liar.' She hated to see him hurting. 'Want me to stick around?'

'What? You're going to cancel a free feed at Marco's to stay here and fight me for the last of the lasagne?' Tris summoned a faint smile. 'Touching, yet stupid.'

'The job went bad, didn't it?'

'I don't want to talk about it, Hal.'

Hallie sighed. He never did. Tris didn't talk about his work for Interpol, ever.

'Go,' he said, waving her away. 'I'm gonna take a shower and get cleaned up. There's nothing you can do. Eat. Be merry.'

And from within the confines of the bathroom as he shut the door behind him, 'Don't talk toothpaste.'

* * *

Nick Cooper always gave a woman fifteen minutes'
grace. Any longer than that and he was inclined to
leave or start without them. Fact was, women enjoyed
keeping men waiting. They did it deliberately to
heighten anticipation and make a man wonder. To
make a man want. All part of the game, but then games
were Nick's specialty. For every attack, there was a
counter-attack, no matter how good your opponent.
And Hallie Bennett's fifteen minutes were almost up.

Not that Nick was even sure she was dining with
him—as she hadn't called—but he'd headed for
Marco's regardless. A man had to eat. And call it a
hunch but he thought she'd show. He browsed the
blackboard specials, scanned the printed menu, looked
around for a waiter and saw instead the delectable
Hallie Bennett heading his way. Her colouring was
pure Renaissance, Titian hair, creamy complexion and
golden brown eyes. But her hair was cropped to chin
length and her face was pure arthouse Animae; all big
eyes, clean lines and memorable mouth.

His body stirred and he narrowed his eyes in an
attempt to conceal the fierce rush of anticipation that
accompanied her arrival as he stood to greet her.
Kissing that smart mouth of hers into submission had
been an absolute pleasure. Getting to know the rest of
her was tempting, very tempting, but the truth was he
couldn't afford the distraction. He didn't need a bed-
mate this coming week; he needed a partner. Someone
with an opportunistic streak, a quick wit, and a deft
touch with the ridiculous.

So far, Ms Bennett had impressed him on all counts.

'Sorry I'm late,' she said when she reached him. 'I wasn't sure I was coming until the last minute.'

'What made you change your mind?' he asked as he saw her seated and tried to ignore the quickening of his breath and of his blood.

'Hong Kong and ten thousand pounds,' she said, her accompanying smile drawing his attention to the generous curve of her lips, currently painted a deep, luscious rose. Her lip colour matched her dress, a sleek, cling-wrap of a dress that emphasized the perfection of the body beneath. 'I like your dress,' he said with utmost sincerity.

'Thank you,' she said, her eyes lightening with a humour that was hard to resist. 'I like it too. Have you ordered?'

'After you.'

She chose the clam chowder. He chose the reef fish and, at her nod, a bottle of white wine to wash it down.

'I'm curious,' she said once that was all settled. 'You're rich, you're handsome, you're healthy—you are healthy, aren't you?'

'Perfectly,' he said, enjoying her candour.

'So why do you need a pretend wife for a week?'

'I'm negotiating distribution rights to a computer game my company has developed. Unfortunately, the distributor's teenage daughter took a liking to me and I found it extremely difficult to, er, dissuade her.'

'You mean you couldn't fend off one fledgling female? You? You're kidding me, right?'

'Wrong.' Nick sighed. He could handle predatory women, honest he could. But a semi-naked eighteen-year-old Jasmine Tey had cornered him in his bed-room late one night, and the sheer unexpectedness of it coupled with more than one glass of his host's most excellent rice wine had rendered him momentarily incapable of sensible thought. 'She was very young,' he muttered defensively. 'Very sweet. I was trying to let her down gently.'

'You invented a wife,' guessed Hallie. 'And now you have to produce her.'

'Exactly. Will you do it?'

'Why not ask a woman you already know to help you out? She'd probably do it for free.'

'Because then I'd have to dissuade *her*. Whereas you and I will have a business arrangement, a contrac-tual obligation if you like, and once you've fulfilled that obligation, you leave.'

'Ah-h-h.'

It was a very expressive ah-h-h.

'Will you and your *wife* be staying with your asso-ciate and his family?'

Nick nodded. 'They have a guest suite. And it's only John Tey and his daughter. He's a widower.'

'Dining with them? Socializing? Getting to know them?'

'All of that,' he said.

Hallie Bennett leaned back in her chair and regard-ed him steadily. 'That's a lot of lies, Nick. Why don't you just tell your distributor the truth? Maybe he'll understand.'

'Maybe.' Nick didn't have a good enough measure of the man to know. When it came to business, John

Tey was cutthroat sharp. When it came to his daughter, the man was putty. 'As far as I can see, John Tey gives his daughter everything she wants.'

'I was raised by my father and four older brothers,' countered Hallie. 'Trust me, giving her what she wants won't apply to men.'

She had a point.

'Unless, of course, your distributor decides that marrying his daughter off to you makes good business sense.'

'Exactly. I can't risk it.' He didn't want to marry Jasmine. He didn't want to marry anyone just yet. And then the bulk of her earlier remarks about her family registered. '*Four* older brothers, you said.'

'Not you too.' Her voice was rich with feminine disdain. 'Would it help if I told you they were all pacifists?'

'Is it true?' he asked hopefully.

'No. But we were talking about you.'

'You're right. I need a wife for a week. Will you do it?' Nick waited as the waiter set their meals in front of them. Waited while she thanked the man, reached for her napkin and set it across her lap, her features relaxed, her expression noncommittal. She was more than he remembered from the shop. More vibrant. More thoughtful. Four brothers.

'I'd need to know more about you than I do now,' she said finally.

'I'll send you a fact file.'

'I'm not a fact-file person.'

Why was he not surprised?

'No,' she continued. 'I'm more of a hands-on person. You're going to have to show me where you live, where you work and what it is you do all day. That kind of thing.'

Nick groaned.

'You can send me the fact file as well,' she said with a placating smile. 'I don't suppose it can hurt. And we're going to need some rules.'

'What sort of rules?' He wasn't very good with rules. Probably not worth mentioning.

'I want physical contact limited to public places,' she said firmly.

'No problem.' His lips twitched.

'And only when we have an audience.'

'You're absolutely right.' At this rate she'd get through every sexual fantasy on his list before dessert. 'What else?'

'I'll follow your lead but only within reason. I won't be a simpering "yes" wife.'

'But you will simper a little?'

Her chin came up; her eyes flashed warningly. 'Can't see it happening.'

'Okay, I can see that simpering might be a stretch for you. Forget the simpering.' He wouldn't. 'Can you do possessive?'

'That I can do,' she said. 'You want the whole hands-off-my-man, slapping routine?'

'No slapping,' he said. 'Ladies don't slap.'

'You never said anything about being a lady.'

Fantasy number three. *Damn* she was good.

'Oh, and there's one more thing…'

'There is?' Every man had his limits and Nick had

just reached his. His brain fogged, his blood headed south and he was thinking leather, possibly handcuffs, although where he was going to get handcuffs from was anyone's guess. Silk, then. No problem finding silk in Hong Kong.

'Earth calling Nick?' said Hallie in exasperation. She'd seen that glazed look before. Knew that Nick Cooper was definitely *not* thinking business. Men! They could never multitask. 'Nick! Can you hear me?'

'Oh, I'm listening.'

He had the damnedest voice. The laziest smile. But this was a business arrangement. Business, no matter how tempting it was to think otherwise. 'My return ticket stays with me.'

CHAPTER TWO

HALLIE couldn't quite remember whose idea it had been to tour Nick's workplace after dinner, only that it had seemed a sensible suggestion at the time. Business, she reminded herself as they stepped from the restaurant out into the cool night air and he slipped his jacket around her shoulders. Strictly business, as she snuggled down into the warmth of his coat and breathed in the rich, masculine scent of him. The fact that his chivalrous gesture made her feel feminine and desirable was irrelevant. So was the fact that he was quirky and charming and thoroughly good company. This wasn't a date, not a real one. This was business.

Nick's office was only a couple of blocks away, familiar territory, this part of Chelsea, and they walked there in companionable silence.

'I need to make a phone call,' she said as Nick halted in front of a classy office block and unlocked the double doors that led through to a small but elegant foyer. 'I'm flatting with one of my brothers at the moment. He's a touch protective; he likes to know where I am if I'm out with someone new. I used to get annoyed with him. Nowadays I just tell him what he wants to know.' Most of the time. She pulled out her mobile and dialled Tris's number, grateful when she got the answering service rather than Tris himself. She relayed her whereabouts and disconnected fast. 'No offence,' she said smoothly.

'None taken. It's a smart move. Makes you a smart woman,' said Nick.

Nice reply.

He ushered her into the lift, the doors closed, and it was intimate, very intimate in there. She cleared her throat, risked a glance. Impressive profile. Big feet. And an awareness between them that was so thick she could almost reach out and touch it, touch him, which wouldn't be smart at all. He turned towards her and smiled that slow, easy smile that bypassed brains and headed straight for the senses, and then—

'We're here,' he said, and the lift doors slid open.

Nick's office suite was a visual explosion of colour and movement. Cartoon drawings covered every inch of available wall space; computers and scanners crammed every desk. There was a kitchenette full of coffee and cola; a plastic trout mounted above the microwave. The whole place was organized chaos and completely intriguing. 'So how many people work here?' she wanted to know.

'Twelve, including me.'

'Let me guess—they're all men.'

'Except for Fiona our secretary. Sadly she refuses to clean.'

'I like her already.'

'Figures,' he said. 'So does Clea. This is my office,' he said, opening a door to a room that was surprisingly tidy.

'What's the basketball hoop for?'

'Thinking.'

Right. 'And the flat-screen TV and recliner armchairs?' There were two chairs, side by side, a metre or so back from the wall-mounted television.

'Working.'

Ah. Why she'd expected a regular office with regular décor was beyond her. There was nothing the least bit ordinary about Nicholas Cooper. 'So tell me more about this game of yours. Is it something I'd know all about if we were married?'

'You'd know about it.' Nick's voice was rich with humour as he slid a disc into the gaming console and gestured towards an armchair. 'If we really had been married these past three years you'd have banned all talk of it by now.'

That didn't sound very wifely. 'Couldn't I have been supportive and encouraging?'

'Sure you could. I was thinking realistically, but we don't have to do that. We can do fantasy instead.'

'Hey, it's your call. You're the fantasy expert. By the way, how long did you tell your distributor you'd been married for?'

'I didn't.' He slid her a glance. 'I'm thinking a couple of months, maybe less. That way if we don't know something about the other it won't seem so odd.'

'Works for me.' And then the game came on. The opening music was suitably raucous, the female figure on the screen impressively funky. 'Very nice,' she said politely. 'What does she do?'

'Mostly she fights.' He handed her a gaming handset. 'Press a button, any button.'

Hallie pressed buttons at random and was rewarded by a flurry of kicks, spins and feminine grunts. Not, Hallie noted, that the figure on the screen even came close to raising a sweat. 'Are those proportions anatomically possible?' she wanted to know.

'Not for earth women,' said Nick. 'Which she's not. Xia here is from New Mars.'

'New Mars, huh? I should have guessed. The clothes she's almost wearing are a dead give-away. Does she have a wardrobe-change option?'

'You want to change her *clothes?*'

'Well, she can hardly kick Martian butt in six inch stilettos, now can she?

He stared.

Hallie sighed. 'You're losing credibility here, Nick.'

'What did you do before you sold shoes?' he wanted to know. 'Bust balls?'

'I worked a blackjack table at a casino in Sydney for a while.'

'Why did you stop?'

'I never saw sunlight.'

'And before that?'

'A brief stint washing dogs in a poodle parlour.' The memory was dim, but still worthy of a shudder. 'Too many fleas.'

'So are you actually trained in anything?'

'I have a fine arts degree, if that counts for anything. And I'm halfway through a Sotheby's diploma in East Asian Art. That's why I came to London.'

'Why East Asian Art?'

'My father's a history professor with a particular interest in dynasty ceramics, and I hung out in his workshop when I was a kid, read all his books.' It had been the crazy-cracks in the glazes that had first captured her interest. The rich history behind each of the pieces had held it.

'So you're following in your father's footsteps. He must be proud of you.'

'No, mostly my father ignores me. I learn anyway. I can spot a fake dynasty vase at fifty paces. In fact I'm absolutely certain the Ming in the Central Museum's a fake.'

He stared.

'All right, ninety per cent certain.'

'So why aren't you finishing your diploma?'

'I will be. Just as soon as I earn enough money for my last two semesters.'

'By selling shoes?'

'It's a job, isn't it?' she said defensively. 'Interesting, well-paid jobs are hard to come by when you're a student. Employers know you're just filling a gap.'

'Couldn't you ask your family to help out?'

'No.' Her voice was cool; he'd touched a nerve. Her brothers would have lent her the money. Hell, they'd wanted to *give* her the money, and so had her father for that matter, but she'd refused them all. Little Miss Independent, and it galled her that they hadn't understood why she'd refused. None of her brothers had taken money from anyone when *they'd* started out. She was staying with Tris because he had a spare bedroom and because London rentals were outrageously expensive. That was all the help she was prepared to accept.

No, money for nothing wasn't her style at all. But ten thousand pounds for a week's work…a week's fairly unorthodox and demanding work… Well now, that was a different matter altogether.

'How much do you need to complete your studies?' he asked curiously.

'Ten thousand pounds plus money to live on. But I've already saved five so with your ten thousand I figure I've got it covered.'

'And then what?' he said. 'Will you roam the world in search of ancient artefacts and long-lost oriental treasure?'

'Yeah, just like Lara Croft and Indiana Jones,' she said, heavy on the sarcasm. 'You know, maybe you need to get out more. You might just be spending too much time in fantasy land.'

'See? I knew it wouldn't take long before you started sounding like a real wife,' he countered with a grin. 'Don't you want to be a tomb raider?'

Sure she did. She just didn't think it very likely. And as for sounding like a nagging wife… Hah! Wait till she really put her mind to it. 'Right now I'm thinking I want to be Xia here, because she's really good at this alien butt kicking business, isn't she? What does she get if she wins?'

'Points.'

'Points as in money? Does she get to shop after-wards?'

'Only for a new weapon.'

'What, no plastic surgery? Because I really think a breast reduction is a must here.'

'Our target demographic is teenage boys.'

'I'd never have guessed.'

'Besides, there's nothing wrong with her breasts—those are excellent breasts. Fantasy breasts.'

Hallie sighed.

'Not that yours aren't very nice too,' Nick added politely.

'Mine are real,' she said dryly, slanting him a side-ways glance. 'Completely real. Just in case anyone should ask.'

'I'm very impressed.' His eyes were blue, very blue, and his smile was pure pirate. 'Because they look to be in excellent shape. I should probably take a closer look; acquire a real feel for them, so to speak. I'm not a fact-file person either.'

'Is your distributor's daughter watching?' she countered smoothly, even as her breasts tingled and her nipples tightened at the thought of him touching her there. 'Are we in a public place?'

'Sadly, no.' And through eyes half closed, his attention back on the screen, 'Man, I love kinky women.'

Oh, boy. 'So what's in this game for us girls?' she said hastily. 'Other than this very cool vibrating controller.'

'Shang.'

'Excuse me?'

'Shang. Paladin princeling.'

Nick flicked back to the main menu and a male figure appeared on the screen. He had dark, carelessly cut hair, an exotic face, a tough, lean body, and was no slouch in the ammunition department either. 'Is that a gun in his pocket or is he just glad to see me?'

Now it was Nick's turn to sigh. 'You're not taking this seriously.'

'It's a game, Nick. I'm not meant to.'

'You're right, you're not. My mistake. *I'm* the one who has to take it seriously. My people have spent three years developing this platform, Hallie, and now it's up to me to market it. I can't afford to make mistakes. Not with John Tey, not with his daughter. That's where you come in.'

'Call me naive when it comes to big business, but I think lying to a potential business partner about your marital status is a mistake,' Hallie felt obliged to point out.

'You sound like my conscience,' he muttered. 'If you have a plan C let's hear it.'

'Ah, well, I don't currently have a plan C.'

'Pity.'

He looked tired, sounded wistful. As if having to deceive John Tey really didn't sit well with him. Sympathy washed over her and all of a sudden she wanted to slide over to his recliner and comfort him. Weave her hands through that dark, tousled hair, touch her mouth to his and feel the passion slide through her and the heat start to build as she feasted on that clever, knowing mouth and—Whoa! Stop right there. Because that wasn't sympathy.

That was lust.

'What?' He was looking at her strangely.

'Indigestion,' she said. 'I think it was something I ate. Probably the clams.'

'Probably the situation,' he said. 'What's it to be, Hallie? Are you in or out?'

Hallie hesitated, tempted to say 'yes'. Not for the adventure, the excitement, or the money, but so that she could spend more time with Nick. The same Nick who was prepared to pay her ten thousand pounds so that at the end of the charade she'd *leave*.

A sensible woman would refuse him now and save herself the heartbreak, the *genuine* heartbreak, that was bound to come if a woman was careless enough to fall for him. A smart woman would sigh over that Hermès handbag, maybe even spend a minute or two imagining what it would look like on her arm, but in the end she'd turn away. That was what she *should* do.

What she said was, 'Do you believe in destiny, Nick? Do you believe in fate?'

'Only as a last resort. Why?'

'I think we should let the game decide. Xia and Shang against the Martians. If we win we go to Hong Kong as man and wife. If we lose, you throw yourself on the tender mercies of Mr Tey and spill your guts.'

'You're serious, aren't you?'

She was.

'Deal,' he said, and the fighting began.

Two murderous hours later it was decided. They were going to Hong Kong.

* * *

Hallie's bedside phone was ringing. She rolled across the bed arm outstretched, groping wildly. Because no way on earth were her eyes going to open at this hour. Her evening with Nick hadn't been a late one by anyone's standards, but it wasn't morning by most people's standards either. It was still dark, not even dawn. She found the phone, found her ear. 'Lo,' she mumbled.

'Can you get some time off work this afternoon?'

'Nick?'

'Yes. Nick.' He sounded impatient.

'Couldn't this have waited till morning?' she mumbled.

'It is morning. Were you still in bed?'

Hallie slitted her eyes open to glance at the glowing red numbers of her bedside clock. Five-fifty a.m! Ugh, he was a morning person. The notion was going to take some time to digest. She held the receiver to her breast and took several deep breaths before putting it back to her ear. 'This is my one day off a week and, I'm warning you, there'd better be a good reason for this call. What do you want?'

'To let you know we have an appointment at Tiffany's at two this afternoon to get your rings.'

'Rings?' Hallie's eyes snapped open. 'Tiffany's? As in Tiffany and Co. the jewellers?' She was wide awake.

'Wedding ring, engagement ring. It'll be expected. The manager of the store on Old Bond Road's a friend of mine; he's going to let me borrow some pieces,' said Nick. 'After that we'll go shopping. You'll need suitable clothes as well.'

Shopping for clothes? This coming from the lips of a man? 'You're gay, aren't you?'

'No,' he said, with a smile in his voice that curled her toes.

'Cross-dresser?'

'Nope.'

'Have you been drinking?'

'Nor am I drunk.' Exasperation in his voice this time, giving her toes a chance to relax. 'The way we present ourselves in Hong Kong is going to be important and I'm guessing there's nothing in your wardrobe that's suitable.'

'Suitable how?' she snapped as visions of tailored suits and pillbox hats floated through her mind. 'You're going to dress me up like Jackie Kennedy, aren't you? You're having make-over fantasies!'

'I wasn't until now.' The smile was back in his voice—yep, there went her toes. 'And I'm not thinking First Lady exactly, but we can't have you looking like Marilyn Monroe either.'

She should have been insulted. Would have been except that this was a sex goddess he was comparing her to. 'Who's paying for these clothes?'

'I am. Consider it a perk.'

'I love this job,' said Hallie. 'I'm in. Two o'clock sharp at the jeweller's. Oh, and, Nick?'

'What?'

He sounded complacent. Indulgent. As if she'd reacted exactly as any good little plaything would. 'Bring your mother.'

* * *

Hallie arrived at the jeweller's at exactly two o'clock, only to find Nick and Clea waiting for her outside, Clea looking thoughtful, Nick looking just plain smug.

'We got here a little early so we've already been in,' said Nick. 'Stuart's given me some pieces on loan. I'm sure you'll like them.'

'What do you mean you're sure I'll like them? You mean I don't even get to go into the shop and ogle the pieces for myself?' Hallie stared at him, aghast. Surely he was kidding. 'Don't you need to measure my ring size or something? I mean, what if the rings you've chosen don't fit?'

'Here, dear, try this on.' Clea handed her one of her own rings, a wide band of square-cut diamonds set in platinum. 'We used this one for size. I usually have a good eye for these things.'

Hallie slipped the band on her wedding-ring finger and stared at it in dismay. It was a perfect fit.

'Does it fit?' asked Nick, all solicitousness. 'It looks like it fits.'

'Sadist,' she retaliated, handing the ring back to Clea, and, with one last lingering glance through the doors of one of London's landmark jewellery stores, she turned away.

'Did you get the week off work?' Nick asked her.

'Yes. The owner's niece is going to fill in for me,' said Hallie, recalling the conversation she'd had with her employer earlier that morning. No need to tell Nick that if the niece liked the job, she was out of one. If everything went to plan she wouldn't need the job anyway.

'What about your brother? The one you're staying with. Does he know you're going to Hong Kong?'

'Not yet. It turns out he's also going to be away next week. I'll leave him a note.'

'That'll go down well,' muttered Nick.

'It'll be fine.' Hallie smiled brightly. 'So where to now?'

Ten minutes later they were standing outside one of the most exclusive clothing boutiques in Knightsbridge. 'Are we sure about this?' said Hallie hesitantly. Buying an outfit or two from a mid-range clothing store was one thing; dropping a bundle on a week's worth of designer clothes was quite another. 'I'm all for being well dressed, but do we really need to shop somewhere quite this exclusive?'

'Don't worry, dear,' said Clea. 'I get a very good discount here.'

'You want to hope so,' Hallie muttered to Nick as she stared at the sophisticated power suit in the display window. 'I think it only fair to warn you that I still have nightmares about the first time my brothers took me shopping for clothes. Pinafore dresses that came to my ankles. Sweaters up to my chin. Wide-brimmed straw hats…'

'And very sensible too, dear, those hats, what with the harsh Australian sun and your skin type,' said Clea.

Hallie groaned. And here she'd been hoping that Clea would be an ally when it came to clothes. 'My point is I battled for years for the right to choose my own clothes, and I'm not about to relinquish it now.' She pointed a stern finger at Nick. 'You can tell me what kind of look you're after, but I won't have you choosing clothes *for* me. Are we clear on that?'

'Well, I—'

'Having said that, I will of course ask your opinion on the things I've chosen. I'm not an unreasonable woman. You can tell me if you like something.'

'And if I don't?'

Hallie considered the question. She could be a bit contrary at times. 'Probably best not to say anything,' she said, and, squaring her shoulders, sailed on into the shop.

The boutique was streamlined and classy, the coiffed and polished saleswoman just that little bit daunting, never mind that she greeted Clea with friendly familiarity.

'Size eight, I think,' said the saleswoman after turning an assessing eye on Hallie.

'Ten,' said Hallie.

'In this shop, darling, you're an eight.'

Hallie liked the woman better already.

'Do you have any colour preferences?' the woman asked.

'I like them all.'

The saleswoman barely suppressed a shudder. 'Yes, dear. But do they all like *you?* Let's start with grey.'

Hallie opened her mouth to protest, but the woman was having none of it. She pulled a matching skirt and jacket from the rack and held them out commandingly. 'Of course, it relies on the wearer for colour and life, but I think you've got that covered.'

'Umm…' Hallie took the suit from the woman and held it up for Nick's inspection. 'What do you think?'

'I'm confused,' he said. 'If I tell you I like it you may or may not decide to buy it, depending on whether *you* like it. However, if I say I don't like it you'll feel compelled to buy it whether you like it or not. Am I right?'

'Yes.' Hallie felt a smile coming on. 'So what do you think?'

'Try it on.'

And then when she did and his eyes narrowed and his face grew carefully impassive. 'No?' she asked. 'It's probably not the look you were after.'

'Yes,' he said firmly. 'It is.'

Still she hesitated. 'It's very—'

'Elegant,' he said. 'Understated. Just what we're looking for.'

Elegant, eh? Not a term she'd normally use to describe herself. She'd won the right to choose her own clothes in her late teens and in typical teenager fashion she'd headed straight for the shortest skirts and the brightest, tightest tops. Okay, so she'd matured a little since then—she did have some loose-fitting clothes somewhere in her wardrobe, but truth was they didn't often see daylight. She had never, *ever,* worn anything as classy as this. The suit clung to her every curve, the material was soft and luxurious beneath her hands, like cashmere only not. Even the colour wasn't so bad once you got used to it. And yet...

'It's not really me, though, is it?' she said.

'Think of it as a costume,' said Nick. 'Think corporate wife.'

'I don't know any corporate wives.' Hallie turned to Clea, who was busily browsing a rack of clothes. 'Unless you're one?'

'No!' said Nick hastily. 'She's not!'

'It's very grey, isn't it, dear?' said Clea, who glittered like a Vegas slot machine in her gold trousers and blood-red chiffon shirt with its strategically placed psychedelic gold swirls.

'Greyer than a Chinese funeral vase,' agreed Hallie glumly. 'Do you have anything a bit more cheerful?' she asked the saleswoman.

'What about this?' said Clea, holding up a boldly flowered silk sundress in fuchsia, lime and ivory. 'This is pretty.'

'Why *my* mother?' muttered Nick. 'Why couldn't we have brought along your mother?'

'She died when I was six,' said Hallie, and then to Clea, 'I like that.' She held it up to her body, twirled around, and looked up to find Nick regarding her intently.

'Sorry,' he said quietly. 'You said you'd been raised by your father and brothers but I didn't make the connection. Try it on.'

And when she did...

'She'll take it,' he told the saleswoman, and to Hallie, 'That's non-negotiable.'

'Lucky for you I happen to agree,' said Hallie.

'His father had excellent taste in clothes as well,' said Clea. 'Bless his soul.'

But Hallie wasn't listening. She was looking at herself in the mirror and her reflection was frowning right back at her as she turned and twirled, first one way and then the other. Finally, hands on hips, she turned to Nick.

'Does this dress make me look fat?'

Two hours later, Hallie and Clea had purchased enough clothes for a six-month stint on the *QEII*, and as far as Nick was concerned he was neither the sadist Hallie had accused him of being, nor the skinflint his mother claimed. No, for a man to endure so much and complain so little, he was quite simply a saint.

'So where to now? Are we done?' said Hallie after they'd seen Clea to her Mercedes and watched her drive away. 'Is there anything *you* need?'

'A bar,' he muttered with heartfelt sincerity.

'Good call,' said Hallie. 'I'll come too. I never realized boutique shopping was such thirsty work. Mind you, I've never bought more than a couple of items of clothes at any one time before either. Who knew?'

'You're not going to rehash every dress decision you just made, are you?'

'Who, me?' She was grinning from ear to ear. 'Only if you insist.'

Nick shuddered, spotted a sports bar a few doors up and practically bolted for the door. He needed a drink, somewhere to sit. Somewhere with dark wood, dark carpet, dim lighting, good Scotch and no mirrors. He needed it bad.

'Ah-h-h,' said Hallie as she slid into the booth beside him. 'Very nice.'

'You don't find it a little too…masculine?'

'Nope. Feels pretty homely to me. I have four brothers, remember?'

'Trust me, I hadn't forgotten. Where do they live?'

'Wherever their work takes them. Luke's a Navy diver midway through a three-year stint in Guam; Pete's flying charter planes in Greece; Jake runs a martial arts dojo in Singapore and Tristan lives here in London. He's the one I'm staying with while I do my course.'

'Tristan?' After Pete, Luke and Jake, a brother named Tristan sounded somewhat incongruous. 'What does Tristan do?'

'He works for Interpol.'

'Paper pusher?'

'Black ops,' she corrected. 'But he's a pussycat really.'

Sure he was. All black ops specialists were pussycats. It was such a caring, non-confrontational profession. 'You know, maybe I need a different type of wife for Hong Kong,' he said. 'Maybe I need a brunette.'

'I was a brunette once,' said Hallie. 'The hairdresser was a young guy, just starting out, and we decided to experiment. He left the salon not long after that.' She sighed heavily. 'I'm sure Tris wouldn't really have castrated him.'

Maybe he was doomed. 'Or a blonde,' he muttered. 'I could always replace you with a blonde.'

'Ha. You can't fool me. You're not going to replace me now; you'd have to go clothes shopping again.'

Nick shuddered. She was right. Replacing her was out of the question.

'Besides,' she continued blithely, 'it's not as if I'm

going to be telling any of my brothers the finer details of our little arrangement. They wouldn't understand.'

On this they were in total accord.

'So tell me about *your* family,' she said, deftly changing the focus back to him and his. 'When did your father die?'

'Two years ago. He was a property developer.'

'And Clea? You said she wasn't a corporate wife. What does she do?'

'Many people find it hard to believe, but she's an architect. A very good one.'

'Is that how they met? Through their work?'

'No, they met at a birthday party. Clea was in the cake. I try not to think about it.'

'What about brothers and sisters?'

'There's just me.'

'Didn't you ever get lonely?' she asked.

'Nope.' She looked as if she was struggling with the only-child concept. 'I had plenty of friends, plenty of company. And whenever I had any spare time there was always a computer handy and a dozen imaginary worlds to get lost in.'

'And now you create fantasy worlds for a living. I guess that means you always knew what you wanted to do, even as a kid.'

'I always did it. Is that the same thing?'

'Probably. My brothers always knew what they wanted to do when they grew up too.' Hallie's smile was wry. 'With me it was different…every week a new idea…astronaut, race-car driver, professional stuntwoman… My family's still not convinced I won't change my mind about wanting to work in the art business.'

'And will you?'

'Who knows?' she said with a shrug. 'I love the thrill that comes with finding something old and beautiful, and I love discovering its history and the history of the people behind it. Hopefully I'll find work with a respectable dealer in Asian antiquities and it'll be fascinating, but if it's not…well…I'll do something else. At least I'll have given it a try.'

'You want to make your own mistakes.'

'That's it!' There was fire in her eyes, passion in her voice. 'Do you have any idea how hard it is to make your own decisions with four older brothers all hell-bent on guiding you through life? I mean honestly, Nick, I'm twenty-four years old and I'm not a slow learner! So what if I make a mistake or two along the way? I'll fix them. I certainly don't need my brothers charging in to straighten me out every time I step sideways.' Hallie's chin came up; he was beginning to know that look. 'I can take care of myself. I *want* to take care of myself. Is that too much to ask?'

'Not at all. What you want is freedom.'

'And equality,' she said firmly. 'And it wouldn't kill them to show me a bit of respect every now and then too.'

Right. Nick quelled the slight twinge of sympathy he was beginning to feel for her brothers and concentrated on the bigger picture. Freedom, equality, respect! He could manage that. It wasn't as if she was asking for the sun, the moon and the stars to go with it.

'I want you to know that even though I'm paying

you a great deal of money to deceive my future business partner you have my utmost respect,' he stated firmly. 'We're in this together as equals.'

And to the drinks waiter who had appeared at his side, 'Two single-malt Scotches. Neat.'

CHAPTER THREE

THREE days later Hallie boarded a plane to Hong Kong. She'd been manicured, pedicured, pampered and polished and was corporate-wife chic in her light-weight camel-coloured trousers and pink camisole. Her shoes matched her top, her handbag was Hermès, and Nick was at her side, thoroughly eye-catching in a grey business suit and crisp white business shirt minus the tie. She was the woman who had it all, and it was all pure fantasy.

That didn't mean she couldn't embrace the moment.

Wispy streaks of cloud scattered the midday sky, their seats were business class, the take-off was perfect, and Hallie relaxed into her seat, prepared to be thoroughly indulged, only to discover that any woman sitting next to Nick was more likely to be thoroughly ignored. That or she was currently invisible to the women of the world as they dimpled, sighed, primped and preened for him.

The flight attendants settled once the flight was underway and went about their business with efficient professionalism, but the encouraging smiles of the female passengers continued. One innovative young lady even managed to trip and fall gracefully into Nick's lap amidst a flurry of breathless apology and a great deal of full body contact.

'Do women always fall over their feet trying to get your attention?' she asked once the woman had gone.

'Actually, she fell over *my* feet,' said Nick. 'They were sticking out into the aisle. It was *my* fault she landed in my lap.'

'And her breasts in your face? That was your fault too?'

Nick shrugged, trying to look a picture of innocence and failing miserably. 'She was trying to get up,' he said in her defence. 'These things happen.'

'So I see.'

He was used to it, Hallie decided. He was just plain used to women falling all over him. 'You know, you'd save yourself a lot of unwanted attention if you wore a wedding ring,' she said. She was wearing one, along with a diamond engagement ring the size of a small egg. As far as the world was concerned she was well and truly taken. Nick's hands, however, were ring-free.

'I wasn't wearing one last time I visited,' he countered. 'It'd seem a bit strange if I turned up wearing one now.'

'No, it wouldn't, considering what happened.' She was beginning to sense some reluctance here. 'Say we really were married, would you wear a ring then?'

'You'd have to insist.' He slid her a sideways glance. 'You would too, wouldn't you?'

'Absolutely.' She held her left hand up between

them, angling her fingers so that the diamond sparkled in the light. 'Some people actually respect the sanctity of marriage and *don't* hit on a person wearing a wedding ring.'

'Funny,' he said dryly. 'You don't look that naive.'

'Hah. It just so happens I don't think I'm *being* naive. But I do concede that if you never wear one we'll never know.'

The clumsy young thing was back, all purring solicitousness as she asked Nick if she'd hurt him, if he was feeling all right, and was there anything, absolutely *anything,* she could do for him.

Honestly!

'Oh, I think we've got it covered.' Hallie smiled, sharp as a blade as her hand—the one with those shiny rings on it—came to rest high on Nick's trouser clad thigh. Nothing subtle about that particular manoeuvre; she was claiming ownership and the other woman knew it. 'On second thoughts, darling, you feel a bit cold,' she said to Nick as she squeezed gently and slid her hand a fraction higher up his thigh. Muscles jumped beneath her palm even as the rest of him went absolutely still. 'Would you like a blanket for your lap? There's one in the webbing in front of you.'

With an annoyed pout and a narrow-eyed glare for Hallie, the other woman made herself scarce. Not that Nick noticed. His *wife* had his attention now. His complete and utter attention.

'What are you doing?' he rasped.

'Practising.'

'For what? The mile-high club?'

Hallie's smile widened. Really, his imagination was so delightfully easy to manipulate. 'I'm practising my possessive moves for when I meet Jasmine.'

'Well, would you mind practising with your hand somewhere else? I'm not made of stone.'

This was debatable. Right this minute, Nicholas Cooper's thigh was hard as a rock. 'Sorry, my mistake. I thought we agreed on physical contact in public places,' she said as she withdrew her hand, reached for the blanket and draped it across his knees. She shouldn't bait him; she knew it. But she couldn't resist. 'This is a public place,' she said sweetly. 'And we did have an audience.'

'You know, you're right. You're absolutely right,' he said. He flicked off the overhead light, brought her hand back to his thigh and drew the blanket over his lap with a smile that was pure challenge. 'Feel free to continue.'

Okay, so there was a slight chance she'd been asking for it. Now *he* was asking for it and she was tempted, very tempted, to deliver. But if she did, things would get out of hand and heaven only knew what would happen after that. Come to think of it, she had a pretty good idea what would happen after that…

And what if they were caught?

They'd be thrown off the plane in disgrace. A big red 'deviant' stamp would appear in her passport and then Interpol would sign her up for sexual misconduct reform school and Tris would find out and, oh, the horror…

Nick wasn't the only one with a vivid imagination.

Feigning nonchalance, Hallie withdrew her hand from his thigh and reached for her glass of water. She was flustered; she was aroused; she was totally out of her league.

She was enjoying every minute of it. 'Actually, I've changed my mind,' she said.

'Good call.' He exhaled deeply.

'After all, it wouldn't do to forget that this is strictly a business arrangement.'

'Exactly.'

Exactly. The sinking feeling in the pit of her stomach was *not* disappointment. Nick was her employer, nothing more, and only for one week. After that it was contract fulfilled and goodbye. Surely she could resist his considerable charms for one lousy week.

All she needed was a more professional approach.

'So how do you want to approach this business of being married?' she said crisply. 'Are we aiming for warm and fuzzy or a fiery attraction of opposites?'

'Think of yourself as a cross between a personal assistant and a German Shepherd,' he said. 'Supportive, loyal, and, when necessary, extremely protective.'

A German Shepherd? Ugh. This new approach worked fast. 'Anything else?'

'Are you sure you couldn't manage a simper?'

'Only if there was a bucket handy. Because I'd probably have to throw up immediately afterwards.'

Nick sighed. 'Just be yourself, then. That'll work too.'

'Oh.' And after a moment's reflection. 'That was a nice thing to say.'

'You realize that was almost a simper.'

'It was not!'

Nick's answering smile was suspiciously gleeful as he flicked on his overhead light, reached for the in-flight paper and snapped it open, effectively ending the discussion.

Hallie glared at the back page of the paper. It was shaking ever so slightly. He was laughing at her, dammit. 'That was *not* a simper.'

'If you say so, dearest.'

A fiery marriage, she decided. A constant battle of words and of wits and it was a damn good thing this marriage was only going to last a week.

Any longer and she'd probably kill him.

Twelve hours and several time zones later, they touched down at Chek Lap Kok International Airport, collected their luggage, and met up with the Teys' driver. They followed the silent Jet Li look-alike through the streamlined arrivals terminal, out through the huge automatic-opening glass doors, and they were in Hong Kong.

'Phew.' Wide-eyed at the sleek steel-and-glass building they'd just emerged from, Hallie paused to gather her composure. 'It's cooler than I thought it would be.'

'It's winter,' countered Nick. 'If you want hot and humid, we'll have to come back in September.'

'Ah.'

They followed the Teys' driver towards an illegally parked Mercedes, and Hallie began to watch him with increasing interest. Maybe it was the way he moved or the way he seemed to know what was happening around them without ever seeming to notice. Maybe it was the way he loaded their suitcases into the trunk as if they were empty, which was definitely not the case. Maybe it was simply that he was gorgeous, with a quiet intensity about him that drew the eye, but…no. That wasn't it either. He reminded her of someone.

He reminded her of Tris.

'*This* is the Teys' driver?' she whispered to Nick. 'I'm guessing that's not all he is.'

'No,' agreed the driver in a soft, cultured voice as he shut the trunk and opened the car door for her. 'I also cook.'

Great. Just what they needed. High-end security with supernatural hearing and a penchant for kitchen knives. Lucky for Nick she'd had years of experience when it came to outwitting suspicious, eagle-eyed men whose mission in life was to serve and protect. At least this one wasn't related to her. 'Pleased to meet you,' she said cheerfully.

'And you, Mrs Cooper.'

Mrs Cooper. Oh, hell. This was it.

For the next five days she was Mrs Nicholas Cooper.

The drive to the Tey residence was a silent one. The driver drove, Nick brooded and Hallie grew wide-eyed again as they entered the neon lit tunnel that would take them beneath Victoria Harbour and across to Hong Kong Island. Awe at the tunnel added to her anxiety about meeting the Teys and set her stomach to churning. Funny, but she'd never actually thought posing as Nick's wife was going to be hard.

Until now.

Finally, they shot out of the tunnel into real light

again, skirted Hong Kong Island's central business district, and started weaving their way up a long, steep slope, towering apartment blocks giving way to luxury villas that grew bigger and grander the higher they climbed.

'How do I look?' she asked as the Mercedes pulled into a paved driveway and swept through no-nonsense wrought-iron security gates that closed behind them.

'Beautiful.' Nick took her hand in his and, with a reassuring smile, brushed her knuckles with his lips. 'You look beautiful.'

'Not helping,' she warned, rapidly withdrawing her fingers from his grasp.

'Beddable,' he said next, which earned him a glare.

They were as ready as they were going to get.

Jasmine Tey was a tiny Asian butterfly with big eyes for Nick. She met them at the door, exquisite in a jewel-coloured sundress, her waist-length black hair held away from her face with a bamboo clasp in a style both youthful and inspired because it drew attention to both face and hair and both were stunning.

'Nick! Welcome,' said Jasmine. 'My father wanted to be here to greet you, but he's been delayed.' She pressed against Nick for a kiss that promised much yet still managed to be just this side of proper.

Hallie grinned and cleared her throat.

'Jasmine.' Nick gently but firmly set her aside. 'I'd like you to meet my wife, Hallie.'

'Hello.' Jasmine's greeting was considerably more subdued than the one she'd bestowed on Nick, but she offered up a small smile nonetheless. 'Nick did not mention you until the end of his last visit. Sadly I thought him available and made a fool of myself.' Her frankness was disarming; the adoring gaze she bestowed on Nick was not.

A few quietly spoken words in Cantonese, uttered by the driver who had come up behind them with their luggage, made Jasmine blush and drop her gaze. 'Kai seems to think I'm still being foolish.'

'Oh, I think you're doing just fine,' said Hallie, glancing speculatively at Kai-the-driver-who-also-cooked before turning back to Jasmine. 'Trust me, the first time I met Nick I almost forgot which way was up. And this woman on the flight today…' Hallie rolled her eyes. 'Why, she practically fell over her feet trying to get his attention. You can imagine.'

A tiny smile tilted Jasmine's lips. It seemed she could.

'I don't blame him,' Hallie continued, warming to her theme. 'He can't help the effect he has on us. Of course, he doesn't have to enjoy it quite as much as he does.'

'But, darling—'

'Don't you darling me, Nicholas Cooper!' He'd wanted possessive, requested jealousy. Hallie had no problem whatsoever delivering both. 'I've had quite enough of women falling over you for one day!' And with a smile for Jasmine, 'I try so hard not to get jealous, but sometimes I just can't help myself. What can I do?'

'You could always try trusting me.' Nick's voice was dry, very dry, as he bent his head and touched his lips to hers in the merest whisper of a kiss.

They were in a public place. They were making a

point for Jasmine's benefit. Role playing, that was all. But the quiet intensity in his gaze made her heart race and her body want for more. Had she really been married to this man she'd want him in her bedroom now. So he could show her with his body and with his eyes just how much he loved her. Not the pretty little flirt on the flight today, not any one of the women who'd tried to engage his interest, but *her*. She was hot, she was sticky, she was well and truly aroused, and dammit she was blushing. 'Um, I don't suppose there's somewhere I can freshen up?' she asked.

'Of course,' said Jasmine. 'Come, I'll show you to your suite. I also have refreshments prepared for you if you'd care to join me on the terrace a little later. I wasn't sure how hungry you'd be so there's a bit of everything.'

Suddenly, Jasmine was as young as her eighteen years, a sweet girl playing hostess for her father and trying hard to do it right. Hallie could relate. 'That sounds lovely,' she said with a warm smile.

Nick's hand was on the small of her back as they followed Jasmine to their suite, the warmth of his touch searing into her through the thin silk of her top. By the time they reached the room his touch was a feather-light caress between her shoulder blades and her body was awash in sensation. 'Right, then, thank you,' she said to Jasmine. 'We'll meet you on the terrace in, um—'

'Half an hour,' murmured Nick in *that* voice, and quietly shut the door.

'Phew.' Hallie blew out a breath and headed for the window, more to put some distance between herself and Nick than to admire the view. It was a magnificent view, though, now that she looked at it. The Teys' three-car garage and manicured, terraced gardens were spread out directly below them and beyond their walls stood more luxury housing that only the extremely wealthy could afford. Downslope, the villas and the apartment blocks gradually morphed into the towering skyscrapers and neon madness of Hong Kong Island's central business district. Beyond that lay the glittering waters of Victoria Harbour and, beyond *that*, more skyscrapers: the skyscrapers of Kowloon. 'Wow,' she said softly.

'Breathtaking, isn't it?' said Nick, crossing the room to stand beside her. 'How do you think it went with Jasmine?'

'She got the point.'

'You don't think it was too subtle?' he asked.

'We women are subtle creatures.'

Nick didn't seem entirely convinced. 'I think we need more.'

'More what? More jealousy? Look, I'm trying to be supportive here, but in my professional opinion you don't want Jasmine thinking you need rescuing from an over-possessive fruitcake.'

'Not more jealousy. More touching.'

Oh.

He slid an arm around her waist and drew her gently towards him. 'Like this.'

This was enough to set every bone in her body to melting. Hallie put her hands to his chest, striving for some distance, even as the lower half of her body betrayed her and settled snugly against him. 'Kai's watching us,' she muttered. He was opening the driver's side door of the Mercedes; maybe he was off to collect John Tey. But he was looking up at them.

'I know.' Nick was hardening against her as they spoke and making no secret of his affliction as his hands slid from her waist to the base of her spine and pressed her even closer.

'Kinky,' she said lightly.

'It may not be the audience.' His lips were curved in a familiar half-smile. 'It could be you.'

She slid her hands to his shoulders, delighting in the feel of him, in the rich, musky scent of his skin. 'You mean you don't know?'

'Nope. And there's not enough blood left in my brain to figure it out.'

'Maybe it's both,' she said breathlessly.

'Now you're trying to confuse me.'

'Actually, I'm trying to distract you.'

'Try harder,' he said, and set his lips to her neck, sending a jolt of pleasure straight through her. Role playing, that was all, but she tilted her head to allow him better access, gasping when the heat of his lips was joined by a whisper of tongue as he teased and tasted his way along her neck.

This was madness, she thought as she buried her hands in his hair and demanded more. Utter madness, as Nick cupped her buttocks and surged against her as his lips rushed over her shoulder, her collar-bone, the swell of her breast, and it was all she could do not to whimper when his mouth found the peak of her breast through the thin layers of silk. All she could do not to scream when his teeth and tongue came into play.

'Nick.' He'd found the clasp on her trousers, his fingers at her waist setting off feathery tremors of sensation. 'Nick! He's gone.'

'Who's gone?' His eyes were black, his breathing was ragged, but comprehension dawned. 'Oh, yeah, him.' His hands stilled, and his big body shuddered as he struggled for control. 'Just give me a minute here.'

No problem. She could do with a minute or two herself. Not to mention a few more metres of unoccupied personal space.

He let her go, let her put some distance between them, but her skin was on fire from his touch and her breasts ached for the feel of his hands and his lips on them again. Half blind with unfulfilled need, she staggered towards the centre of the room. And stopped.

The floor was the palest marble streaked with grey. The furniture was intricately carved cherry wood inlaid with mother of pearl. The furnishings were red. Not dull red, not blood-red, but a bright primary-colour-wheel red. The floor rug, the drapes, the bed…yes, indeed, the bed was undeniably red, with enough cushions and pillows piled against the headboard to furnish a small orphanage.

'I thought you said there was a sofa as well,' she said at last.

'There was,' said Nick, frowning. 'It used to be over by the far wall.'

Well, there certainly wasn't one there now. Nothing in this room but a bed. A big red bed.

'The Chinese consider red a fortuitous colour,' said Nick. 'It's supposed to bring good luck.'

'Good,' she muttered. Because they were definitely going to need it if they were going to be sharing that bed. 'Mind if I take first shower?'

'Go ahead.' Nick gestured towards a door to her right.

The bathroom was marble too, all marble, with gold taps, red towels and the biggest glass-walled shower cubicle she'd ever seen. *Two* shower rosettes in that cubicle. Two of them, side by side, commanding her attention the way the bed had in the other room.

'Or we could shower together and save time,' he said from the doorway.

Did he honestly think that getting wet and naked with him was going to save time? She slid him a glance. He was leaning against the doorframe, his smile crooked and his eyes dark.

No, he didn't think that either.

Nick knew women. Knew the feel of them in his arms and in his bed. More than that, he liked women and they could generally be counted on to like him right back. But he'd never met a woman who affected him the way Hallie Bennett did. Hell, when she was in his arms it was all he could do to recall his own name, let alone the terms of their agreement.

So she was amusing…women often were.

So she was beautiful…there were plenty of women out there who were that too.

But since when had he ever wanted to watch a woman's face for ever, just so he wouldn't miss whatever she came out with next? Since when had a woman ever distracted him from his work and his goals for the company? Since when had a woman ever had *that* kind of power over him? Since never, that was when. And he didn't like it, not one little bit.

Hallie Bennett was here to *solve* his woman problems, not cause more.

By the time she emerged from the bathroom, sleek and elegant in a moss-green sheath, he was thoroughly riled. It didn't help that he knew he was being unreasonable, that she'd only been doing what they'd agreed on in the first place. It certainly didn't help that she took one look at him and judged his mood in an instant.

'Pick a topic, any topic,' she said airily. 'Religion, politics, whatever you like. I'm sure we can come to a disagreement about something.'

'Sport,' he said abruptly. There wasn't a woman of his acquaintance who could talk sense when it came to sport.

'Of course, there's only one real sport and that's soccer,' she stated firmly.

'Football,' he corrected.

'Whatever. I favour Brazil, myself.'

'Because they win?'

'No.' Her eyes narrowed thoughtfully. 'I'm pretty sure it has something to do with the green and gold uniform.'

'You support Brazil because of the colour of their *shirts*?' Now they were getting somewhere. 'That's ridiculous.'

'Would you rather I supported them because they're fascinating to watch and consistently produce some of the finest strikers in the world?'

'Er, no. That would defeat the entire purpose of the conversation. I'm trying to find something to dislike about you.'

'Ah.' And with a very sweet smile. 'About the shower… I'm afraid I used all the hot water.'

'Hmph.' Even that wasn't a problem, he thought glumly as he gathered up his shaving kit and stalked towards the bathroom. A cold shower was just what he needed.

The shower helped. Helped enough so that when they went downstairs Nick was cool, calm and back in control. He could do this. *They* could do this. It was far too late to back out now. They *had* to do this.

John Tey arrived home from work with Kai at his side just as they stepped onto the terrace so it was introductions all round with Hallie making all the right noises: assuring their host that Jasmine had made them more than welcome in his absence, that the trip had not been at all tiring and that, yes, she was definitely looking forward to her stay, and delivering it all with such warm approachability that John Tey didn't stand a chance.

Within five minutes she'd discovered that their host clipped his own hedges and spent an hour every morning practising t'ai chi. That he owned an extensive art collection and that Jasmine was an accomplished silk painter. Five minutes and Jasmine was giggling, John was smiling, and even the po-faced Kai had relaxed his guard, and it was all Hallie's doing as she charmed them with her warmth, wit and enthusiasm for life. Whatever the moment held, she embraced it; be it a computer game or a kiss, she gave it everything she had.

Damn but the woman could kiss.

'Do you collect antiquities?' John asked her as she bent to examine a little jade horse set on a marble pedestal.

'My father does. John, this is exquisite. Early Qing dynasty, isn't it? I've never seen one in such good condition.'

Nick blinked at her knowledge of little green horses. John beamed at the compliment.

'Kai will drive you to some of our smaller private galleries in the morning if you wish. There you will find many beautiful pieces. Perhaps even a memento of your stay with us.'

'Perhaps.' Hallie smiled easily, her glance encompassing them both. 'I don't want to disrupt any plans you have in place but I'd love to see the New Year decorations in the city as well. And the lion dancing… Maybe buy some oranges…'

Jasmine was nodding her head in vigorous agreement. John's gaze was wry as it rested on his daughter.

'My daughter has also suggested she show you these things. Would tomorrow be suitable?' And to Jasmine, 'You will let Kai know when you wish to leave.'

'But, Father, surely we can go alone.'

'No.' It was the first time Nick had ever seen him refuse his daughter anything.

'But, Father—'

John Tey held up his hand and there was instant silence from Jasmine.

'Kai will accompany you.'

Jasmine bent her head in acquiescence. 'Yes, Father.'

'So it is settled.' John was back to playing charming host. 'Come, Nick. You must try the spring rolls. Jasmine makes them herself.'

As far as Hallie was concerned the evening passed pleasantly and far too quickly, the problem being that as soon as they retired for the evening she and Nick would have to confront that big red bed. The sofa was gone, that much was certain, and the floor was made of marble. *She* certainly wasn't going to sleep on a marble floor, nor did she expect Nick to. No, they were going to have to share the bed and somehow she was going to have to keep her hands to herself.

So she was slightly nervous as they headed for the guest suite, slightly bug-eyed as he followed her into their room, loosening his tie as he closed the door before automatically proceeding to the buttons of his shirt. Habit, that was all; there was nothing sexual about it. But she couldn't let him continue.

'Bathroom,' she said sternly, pointing the way.

'Right.' Nick scooped up his toiletries and headed for the bathroom without another word.

One week. Be professional. She could do this.

Hallie's gaze slid to the bed.

How on earth was she going to do this?

By the time he'd finished in the bathroom and Hallie had had her turn and slipped into her Mickey Mouse singlet and boxers-for-girls she had it figured. Fortunately, Nick wasn't in bed yet. He was standing at the window, a dark silhouette against the night sky, and if she thought he looked good in a suit it was nothing compared to what he looked like in tight black boxers.

'I'll take the floor,' he said.

'You can't take the floor. The floor is too hard. Anyway, I have a plan.' Hallie strode over to the bed and began stacking cushions straight down the middle of it.

'*This* is your plan?' he asked, somewhat sceptically.

'*This*,' she said, busily stacking cushions, 'is the Great Wall of China. You are the Mongol horde and I am the Emperor's finest troops.'

He looked as if he wanted to laugh, caught her glare, and must have decided against it.

'Well, that hardly seems fair,' he said finally. 'Why can't I be the Emperor's finest and *you* be the barbarians?'

'Fine. Just stay on your side of the wall, okay?'

'I will defend this wall with my very life.'

'Whatever.' That'd teach her to mix metaphors with a computer games master. She slipped beneath the covers and lay down. Moments later Nick approached the bed and the mattress dipped as he lay down. Her plan was working. And then Nick's head and torso appeared above the cushions, his elbow skewing them haphazardly.

'The Emperor's troops are allowed on the wall, right? I feel like I should be patrolling it.'

'Trust me, you don't have to patrol the wall. There is nothing happening on your northern border tonight. Get some sleep.'

He disappeared behind the wall of pillows only to return again almost immediately.

'No raiding party?'

'No. There is nothing on your side of the wall that the barbarians want.' This was a lie. She knew for a fact that there were enormous treasures to be found just a cushion's length away.

'Here's the problem,' said Nick. 'I've never slept in the same bed with a woman and not *slept* with her, if you get my meaning. I feel like I should be doing something.'

'Go to sleep. Think of the wall.' She, however, would be spending the rest of the night fantasizing about what it was he thought he should be doing.

'Have *you* ever slept with a man and not slept with him?' he asked.

'Yes.' Did sharing tent space on a camping trip with a nine-year-old brother count? 'It's not hard.'

'Wrong,' he said. 'It's extremely hard. A raiding party would know this already.'

Hallie's stomach clenched and her toes curled as she tried not to picture in vivid detail exactly which part of Nick was hard. 'Sending a raiding party over that wall would be suicide,' she countered.

'What if I invited you over for peace negotiations?'

'Hah! I'm not falling for that old trap.'

'I can't believe you ever thought this plan was going to work,' he said as the bottom-most pillow tumbled from the bed.

'Fine then. I'll sleep on the floor.'

'You can't sleep on the floor. The floor is too hard.'

'Then go to sleep before I strangle you,' she yelled. And after a moment's reflection, 'You're deliberately inciting the Mongol horde, aren't you?'

'Is it working?'

'No.' She punched the pillow at her head until it was shaped to her liking and deliberately turned her back to him. 'The Mongol horde is wise to your tricks.'

She heard his low, sexy chuckle followed by the rustle of sheets.

'Goodnight, Mrs Cooper.'

And much, much later, when the regular, even rhythm of his breathing told her he'd fallen asleep, 'Goodnight, Nicholas.'

CHAPTER FOUR

NICK woke before the dawn with a sleeping Hallie snuggled tightly into his side. Her head was on his shoulder, her arm was resting on his chest, her legs were entwined with his, and there wasn't a pillow in sight. What was more, he noted with no little satisfaction, she was on his side of the bed, *his,* which meant that, technically, *she* was the one doing all the invading. Her body was relaxed, her breathing slow and even. The Mongol horde was vulnerable. Question was: what was he going to do about it?

A gentleman would slide on out of bed without waking her and head for the shower. A rogue would wake her with kisses, slide on into her, pleasure her until she was sated, then *carry* her to the shower. Tough choice.

He was still debating tactics when he felt her stir. Her long, smooth legs tangled even more closely with his and her hand traced a leisurely path from his chest to his stomach sending a shiver of pleasure straight through him. Even in sleep she knew just what to do to get his undivided attention. And then she stopped.

Nick felt her body stiffen, heard her sharply indrawn breath. She was awake.

'Morning,' he said huskily, although at this hour, with silvery darkness still enveloping them, that was debatable. She jerked up on one elbow, looked around wildly, and her knee connected with his crotch. 'Oomf!' His eyes crossed. His breath left his body. So much for his wake-up sex fantasy.

'Sorry,' she muttered, removing her knee and patting him better abstractedly. 'What happened to the pillows?'

'Try the floor,' he wheezed as the patting continued. Was this heaven or hell? He couldn't decide. He levered himself up on his elbow and looked over the side of the bed. 'Yep. There they are.'

'Oh.' She stared at him and all of a sudden the hand on his crotch stilled.

'You're leaning on your elbows,' she said.

'So?'

'So if your arms are *there,* my hand is—'

He watched her eyes grow round and her cheeks grow rosy with no little satisfaction.

'That's not your arm I'm patting, is it?'

'Nope.' Nick settled back against the headboard, amused, aroused and altogether curious as to what she'd do next. 'It's not.'

The colour in her cheeks had spread to her chest, her nipples had pebbled against the thin cotton of her singlet. Her eyes were downcast, hiding her expression. But it was her hand that held his attention. Because it hadn't moved.

'I didn't think ones this size were real,' she said finally. 'I thought they were an urban myth.'

'This one's real,' he said, almost groaning as her hand crept along his shaft towards the tip.

'Have you measured it?'

He was male. Of course he'd measured it. 'It's not that big,' he said reassuringly. 'Don't let it frighten you.'

'Ha! Easy for you to say.' She reached the tip, curled her hand around him and started slowly back down. 'It's got to be at least nine inches long,' she said accusingly.

'Not quite,' he corrected, unable to stop himself from arching up into her hand with a groan of pure pleasure. He was still playing the gentleman, heaven help him he was, but a man could only take so much. She was driving him mad. He couldn't see her eyes, couldn't figure what she wanted. He, however, was absolutely certain about what *he* wanted. He put his hand beneath her chin—that determined little chin—and brought her gaze up to meet his. Her eyes widened. There was uncertainty in her eyes and curiosity too—he was used to both from the women who shared his bed, but it was desire he looked for. Desire he found.

His gaze fastened on her mouth as he drew her closer, close enough to bend his head and set his lips to hers, every whisper of a touch, every leisurely rub, maddeningly erotic and not nearly enough. He wanted more, demanded it with a nip to her bottom lip so she'd open for him and damn near lost control when she did. He couldn't get enough of her taste and her texture, couldn't get enough of that soft, lush mouth against his own. He broke the kiss with a groan, craving more, much more, and needing to know he could take it. 'I want to be inside you, Hallie. All the way inside,' he murmured huskily. 'Is that what you want?'

'I'm not sure. I think so,' she whispered, and Nick groaned.

'"I think so" is not good enough,' he muttered, even as he slid his hands around her waist and urged her slim body closer, a shiver of response rippling through him as her legs tangled with his and her breasts pressed against his chest. 'You have to say "yes".'

'Yes.'

Lord but she was sweet as her hands slid to his shoulders as she rolled with him to the middle of the bed, wanting him above her, over her, straining against him with incoherent little mutterings that lit his blood. Beautifully wanton as she lifted her arms above her head, helping him to remove her top, and then her hands were on him again as she wrapped her arms around his neck and dragged him down for another of those soul-stealing kisses. He felt her shudder, felt her arch up into him, her urgency igniting his own.

He wanted to make sure she was prepared for him—he *always* made sure a woman was ready for him—but with Hallie what he wanted and what he needed were two completely different things. He wanted to pleasure her. But he needed to be inside her, buried in her up to the hilt, taking him all…dammit, she drove him to madness. His hands were fast and urgent as he slid her tight little boxers from her body, and then shed his own, his need for her clawing at him as he spread her thighs wide and positioned himself between them. He found her with the head of his penis, found her wet and warm and tight.

And she froze.

No! His soundless roar of protest came from somewhere deep and primitive within. No! He wouldn't let her stop now. Couldn't. So he rolled with her until she was on top of him, nestled against him. It was the best he could do. 'We can go slow,' he muttered, knowing even before he heard himself speak that his voice would be harsh and strained.

She pushed herself into a sitting position, her face flushed and her breath coming fast. 'I don't think I can do this.'

'Really slow,' he said. And turned his considerable will towards proving that he could.

Gentle, as he cupped her hips and positioned them so that she dragged against him. Slow, as he rocked back and forth, watching, always watching, to see that what he was doing pleased her. And, heaven help them both, she was easy to please.

'Nick, I— Oh…'

He licked at her nipple, flickered his tongue back and forth across that hard little bud. So easy to please as he grazed her with his teeth and soothed her with his tongue before taking her breast more fully into his mouth and suckling hard. She arched back at that, whimpering her approval before demanding he pay attention to her other breast. He could do that. Did exactly that as his hands skittered down her spine and then she was wresting that breast from him and devouring his lips with her own, each nip, each slide of that clever, honeyed mouth dragging him deeper.

'Work with me here,' he muttered. 'I'm pretty sure I can go slower. You just have to stop kissing me like that.'

'Oh, my God!' she said.

He nipped at her jaw, the slender curve of her neck, the sweep of her shoulder, and everywhere he touched she responded with a shudder, a purr, a gasp. He was dizzy with the feel of her, wild with need for her. He slid his fingers between her legs, found her soft and damp as he parted her protective folds to expose her tiny bud and position himself against her more fully. Against but not in, always rocking, always intensifying the sweet slide of skin against skin until her breath came in short, sharp gasps and her eyes turned molten. Her fingers dug into his shoulders, her mound slick and swollen against his hardness as her movements grew more frantic. He sucked in his breath as she trailed her hands down his chest to his nipples and stroked them to hardness, carefully passive, and aching with the control it took to stay that way as she moved her hands lower, positioned herself above him and guided him in, a fraction at a time.

That was when he felt it. A barrier in his way.

No! Surely not. It couldn't possibly be what he thought it was. Could it? Her eyelashes were shielding her eyes, her brow was furrowed as she focussed intently on the task at hand and, dammit, she was chewing on her bottom lip. Oh, no. Please, no. 'You're not a virgin, are you?' he asked with an impending sense of doom.

'Does it matter?' she said, still trying—unsuccessfully—to accommodate him.

What did she mean, did it matter? 'Of course it matters!' he roared. 'Oh, hell. You *are* a virgin!'

'Well, technically, yes,' she admitted. 'But I'm not *that* inexperienced. I've had sexual relations before.'

'Don't you dare bring politics into this conversation,' he snapped, snatching his hands from her body and pressing them against the bed as he struggled for control. 'You! A virgin! What next?'

Her eyes narrowed, her chin came up. He loved that look. His *body* loved that look. His body, he thought with increasing alarm, was almost past the point of stopping.

'Get off,' he ordered.

'You've got to be kidding me.' She bit her bottom lip, pressed down hard, and suddenly, suddenly, he was in.

Her eyes watered, her breath seemed to catch in her throat.

Oh, God! His control was moments away from shattering. She was so hot, so tight, so *wet*. 'Don't panic!' he muttered. 'We can fix this.'

How on earth were they going to fix this?

Hallie started to giggle.

'Don't laugh,' he ordered. 'Don't move!' If she moved, he was history.

She moved, and so did he, rolling with her, rolling her onto her back and moving over her, into her, his movements carefully restrained as he tried, God help him, to be gentle with her.

She looked up at him then, her eyes dark and slumberous and her lips curved, and he felt her melt into him,

felt her body grow accustomed to him as his strokes
grew longer until at last he was sheathed inside her completely. He managed a smile, shuddering with the effort
it took to rein himself in. 'You okay?' he muttered.

'Absolutely.'

And then she was threading her hands through his
hair and dragging his lips down to hers and he was
surging into her, his control a thing of the past. Trying
to be gentle with her and not at all sure he was suc-
ceeding as he rode out his need for her, his fascination
with her, each stroke destroying him, what was left of
him, and all around them was the rich scent of sex and
the slide of sweat-slicked bodies. His need for her was
outrageous, his satisfaction darkly overwhelming as
she gave herself over to him, came for him, convulsing
around him with a soft, sexy cry that screamed through
his senses.

Now. As she cried out again, wrapped her legs
around him and urged him deeper.

Now.

Later, much later, he carried her to the bathroom,
turned the shower on hot and hard and stood her under
the spray, one arm wrapped around her waist to support her. Gentleman or rogue—he figured he had his
answer. Figured he was going to have to live with it.
'Can you stand?' he asked gruffly.

'Of course I can stand.' She pushed his arm away
and took a couple of wobbly steps towards the soap.
'Walking's the challenge.'

'Here…' He adjusted the showerheads so that the

water cascaded over them both and handed her the soap. He'd never in his wildest dreams imagined that sassy Hallie Bennett was a virgin. She was twenty-four. What woman in this day and age reached her mid-twenties still a virgin? And why? 'I, ah, hope you weren't saving yourself for your future husband,' he said awkwardly.

'I wasn't.' Hallie's lips twitched as she started soaping herself down. 'Don't panic, Nick. I was a virgin, yes, but I was ready for that to change. I'm not out to trap you.'

That was a relief. Until a new and wholly unwelcome thought occurred to him. Whether she was out to trap him or not they'd just had unprotected sex. He'd never been so careless with a woman before. Ever! What if she fell pregnant and had a child? His child. There was no way any child of his was going to grow up without a father and, as far as Nick was concerned, that meant marriage. His blood turned to ice; his breath caught in his throat. What had he done?

'Are you okay?' she asked him. 'You don't look so good.'

'I, ah, guess it's unlikely you were protected against pregnancy, what with you being a virgin and all.' He was being wildly optimistic, he knew he was.

'Actually, I *am* protected,' she said. 'That's something we don't have to worry about.'

The breath left his body in a whoosh. Regular breathing resumed.

'Call it a complete stab in the dark,' said Hallie dryly, 'but I'm guessing marriage and children aren't on your to-do list.'

'I, uh…' He was still recovering, still trying to regroup. 'No, they're on the list,' he said at last. 'They're just not at the *top* of the list at this point in time.'

'Ah.' She smiled. 'Good to know.' And from beneath lowered lashes, 'For what it's worth, I think you're an incredible lover. I'm glad you were my first.' Then she lifted her face to the water and put her hands to her hair in a move so innately sensual he felt the force of it like a punch to his stomach.

Definitely not part of the plan, he thought as he dragged her up against him with a muffled curse. And took her again.

Nick soaped up beneath the spray as Hallie stepped from the shower and wrapped herself in a towel. She slid him a dreamy smile, followed up with a stern warning for him to keep his distance, as she padded from the bathroom. Not a problem, he thought wryly, because, frankly, he was spent.

Lovemaking had always been a pleasurable pastime for Nick. Sometimes it was slow and lazy, sometimes quick and playful. This time had been different. This time his climax had ripped through him like a tornado, leaving him dazed and shaken. And worried.

So what if she was a generous lover?

So what if towards the end there he'd hardly known who or where he was, only whom he was with? It wasn't as if he'd found The One. Hell, he was only thirty; he was far too young for that. He had years and years of loving left in him before *that* happened.

Yeah, whispered his brain. Years and years of

mediocre bed play that will never, *ever* measure up to what you've just experienced with Hallie Bennett.

'No,' he said fiercely.

Oh, yeah, throbbed his heart. Years and years spent searching for another Titian-haired, golden-eyed witch whose smile warms you through and whose kisses make your soul tremble.

'No!' Louder this time. This was not happening. Regardless of her sweetness, her savvy, and her thorough understanding of football, Hallie Bennett was definitely *not* The One.

He wouldn't let her be.

She was lying on her stomach on the freshly made bed, leafing through the travel guide to Hong Kong he'd given her, when he finally emerged from the bathroom. Her trouser-clad legs were bent at the knees, her dainty little feet—clad in strappy little sandals—were crossed at the ankles. Her arms were bent at the elbows, her collared shirt showed a modest amount of cleavage. She looked casual, comfortable and perfectly at ease. Perfectly approachable, which was good because he was about to re-establish the boundaries of their relationship.

Just as soon as he put some clothes on.

She looked up at him and smiled as he crossed to the wardrobe and there was lazy satisfaction in that smile, a woman's awareness. His doing, his alone, for there'd been no one else before him and damned if he didn't relish the notion.

No way. No. This was *not* happening.

He turned his back on her and dressed fast, deliberately avoiding her gaze as he headed for the sideboard and his business papers.

'I've been thinking,' he said gruffly.

'It shows.'

He shot her a glance, darkly amused. 'I've been thinking we should stick to the plan from now on.'

'Fine.'

'I mean, the whole point of bringing you along was so that this kind of complication *wouldn't* crop up.'

'I know.'

'We got a bit carried away, that was all. A body has its needs.'

She smiled at that and he had the uncomfortable feeling that she'd anticipated each and every one of his defences.

'I promise it won't happen again,' she said, and it was all he could do to keep his jaw from hitting the ground. 'That's what you want to hear, isn't it?'

Well, yes. It was just that he wasn't expecting to hear it quite so readily. Where was the dismay? The protest at having to give up such incredible lovemaking? The businessman in him was relieved. The lover was insulted. The lover, he thought darkly, was the one who'd got him into this mess in the first place. 'I think we need a new rule,' he said firmly. 'No more sex.' And then as she sat upright, slid on over to the edge of the bed and winced as she did so, 'How are you feeling?'

'Tender,' she confessed, blushing to the roots of her hair. 'I don't think I'm going to have any problem complying with your new rule.'

Great. Just Great. Now he had guilt. This, he remembered grimly, was one of the reasons he'd never taken a virgin to his bed. He didn't know what to do. How to help. 'Maybe you should take it easy today, postpone your sightseeing trip. I'm sure Jasmine wouldn't mind.'

'I'd mind,' said Hallie. 'I want to see the galleries.'

So much for trying to get her to rest. What was it with women and shopping? Which reminded him. He sifted through his computer case for his spare cash; found it at the very bottom of the case, beneath the computer. 'Here,' he said, holding it out towards her. 'Take it. You might see something you want to buy at the shops today.'

Hallie stared at the thick wad of money, stared at him. 'I thought we agreed you'd pay me at the end of the week.'

Nick nodded. 'And I will. This is just shopping money.'

'Shopping money.' She said it slowly, looking at the money as if it were poison. Looking at him as if he were a snake. 'Keep it,' she said, with a bite in her voice that was new to him.

'Look, you're going to the galleries,' he said, thoroughly baffled by her reaction. 'I'm assuming that whatever they sell there won't come cheap and, if I know Jasmine, she'll consider your outing a failure unless you find something you can't resist. I certainly don't expect you to use your own money for that kind of thing. Put it in your handbag just in case.'

'No!' She sounded fierce, looked fragile. 'I know

you're paying me to pretend to be your wife, and I know I let you buy me clothes for the trip, but you can keep your *shopping* money. I won't take it.'

'Why not?' The way he saw it, it was all part of the same deal.

She looked away. 'Because it'd make me feel like even more of a whore,' she said finally.

Nick blinked. Then he scowled. 'Don't be ridiculous!' Okay, so his timing could have been better. He shouldn't have offered her money so soon after sex. But she'd seemed just fine about the sex, he thought morosely. Not to mention the ceasing of it. They'd finished that discussion, hadn't they? And moved on. 'This money's got nothing to do with the sex!' he snapped. 'Don't you dare think I'm trying to pay you for sex!'

She looked slightly mollified. A little uncertain. But her chin was high. 'I'm still not taking it.'

Then they were at an impasse. Because Nick was equally determined that she would. 'What if I commissioned you to buy me a gallery piece while you were out shopping today?' he said. 'What if I secured your professional services as an antiquities expert, so to speak? Would that be acceptable?'

'I'm listening,' she said warily.

'Buy me something.' He tossed the money down on the bed beside her.

'With this much money I could probably buy you Hong Kong Harbour,' she said in a small voice, staring down at the notes scattered across the bedspread. 'What do you want?'

'You're the expert. You choose.'

'Yes, but a buyer usually has *some* idea what their client is after.'

Buyer and client now, were they? He should have been pleased that she was going to take the money. He should have been happy she'd finally come to her senses and recognized it as a necessary part of the charade rather than some kind of postcoital pay-off, but he didn't feel pleased. He felt...hollow. 'Buy me a vase,' he said. It was the first thing that came to mind.

'Fine. A vase it is.'

He watched her shove the notes into a zippered section of her handbag, smile a bright false smile and head for the door. Something was bothering him. Something big.

'You didn't really think I'd treat you like a whore, did you?' he asked quietly.

She didn't answer.

CHAPTER FIVE

THERE was something to be said for being chauffeur-driven around Hong Kong in a Mercedes, decided Hallie two hours later as Kai expertly negotiated the traffic with the ease of long familiarity. Jasmine sat beside her in the back seat, cheerfully pointing out places of interest, from museums to major corporations, the Bird Garden to the Goldfish Market. Any other day and Hallie would be embracing the opportunity to shop for antiques with a knowledgeable guide and a chauffeur to boot, but not today. Today her mind was on Nick and his lovemaking. More specifically, on what had happened afterwards.

Good Lord, what a mess.

She'd been expecting Nick to pull back after their lovemaking. She'd started preparing for it the minute she'd stepped from the shower, and she'd been doing all right as they'd re-established the rules of their relationship. She'd been doing pretty well considering that this had been her first morning-after ever. Very well considering her feelings for Nick weren't nearly as casual as she'd made them out to be.

And then he'd acted all concerned for her well-being, and she'd let her guard down and allowed herself to believe, just for a moment, that she meant something to him. That he'd found their lovemaking as incredible as she had. And then he'd offered her the shopping money, and, boy, hadn't she taken *that* the wrong way? Hallie leaned her head against the window-pane, closed her eyes, and tried to wish it all away. The lovemaking, the misunderstanding, the money…

The sooner she got rid of the money weighing down her soul and her handbag, the better.

'Hallie, are you okay?'

Hallie straightened up, opened her eyes, and smiled at the younger girl who was looking across at her in concern. 'I'm fine. Just a little tired.'

'Did you not sleep well? Was the bed uncomfortable?'

'No, no. The bed was very comfortable.' Sharing it was the problem. 'It's probably jet lag kicking in. I'll be okay. Really.' With a determined breath she focussed on the younger girl and their outing. 'So tell me, where's your favourite place in the whole city?' she asked.

'The Lucky Plaza food hall,' said Jasmine promptly. 'They have the finest selection of food in the city. You can try a little of everything! I usually do.'

'We could go there for lunch,' said Hallie.

Jasmine looked uncertain.

'Your father would not approve of your choice of eating venue,' said Kai in his quiet, implacable way.

'I'll ask him,' said Jasmine, lifting her chin in a

defiant gesture that was vaguely familiar. A quick conversation on her mobile and it was done. 'He said yes,' she told Kai sweetly.

Hallie watched with interest as Kai's gaze clashed with Jasmine's in the rear-view mirror, his stony, hers limpid. It was like water meeting rock; the rock endured but the water was fluid and tricky, not to mention flawlessly beautiful and surprisingly strong-willed. Jasmine held Kai's gaze in silence until finally he turned his attention to the road. The smile Jasmine slid Hallie was impish. Hallie returned it in full.

'So when would you like to eat?' asked the younger girl. 'One o clock?'

Lucky Plaza was a well-maintained seventies shopping complex. Inside was clean and nondescript with a worn look that spoke of many feet. Nothing special, thought Hallie, until they reached the food hall and she discovered that here was where the people of Asia came together to celebrate food.

'See? I knew you would like it,' said Jasmine, accurately judging her fascination. And to Kai, 'And she hasn't even tried the food yet.'

He steered them towards an empty table in a corner and sat them down unceremoniously, his gaze not on Jasmine but on two dark-suited Asian gentlemen standing by a nondescript staircase some twenty metres away. 'Stay here,' he told Jasmine.

'Go,' Jasmine waved him away. 'We shall make our food selections while we wait for you.'

Hallie watched as Kai strode towards the staircase,

according the staircase sentries the barest of nods before taking the stairs. 'So what's with the sentries?' she asked. 'Where's Kai going?'

'To pay our respects,' said Jasmine. 'One does not enter another's territory without observing the formalities.'

'What territory? You mean Triad territory?'

'Oh, no,' said Jasmine hastily. 'Kai would never allow us to go *there*. Lucky Plaza is owned by another of Hong Kong's criminal organisations. They are…less than Triad but still worthy of respect. You can see why I had to ask my father if it was appropriate to bring you here.'

Yes, well, she did *now*. So much for thinking Kai's objection to the lunch venue was a simple power play. 'How long has Kai been with you?' she asked.

'Almost ten years. Ever since my mother was killed during an attempted robbery at a fuel station. I don't think my father ever forgave himself for not taking better care of her.' Jasmine sighed. 'He's determined to take better care of me.'

'I know the feeling,' said Hallie. 'My mother died of cancer when I was six. My father grieved and retreated into his work so my older brothers took on the task of raising me. I have four of them.'

'*Four* older brothers,' said Jasmine in fascinated horror. 'Were they protective of you?'

Hallie nodded. 'They still are. It drives me insane.'

'But surely now you're married they would expect Nick to assume the role of protector,' said Jasmine.

Oh, yeah. She'd forgotten about Nick, her *husband*.

'Well, yes,' she said awkwardly. Lord only knew if her brothers would change their ways if she really were married. No potential suitor, upon meeting all four of them, had ever been brave enough to stick around.

'He looks to be a wonderful husband,' said Jasmine with a wistful sigh.

Who? Nick? Hallie suppressed a nervous giggle. Who knew? 'Nick's deceptive,' she said finally. 'He gives me the freedom to make my own mistakes.' Like making love to him that morning. 'But when you get down to it, he's a lot like my brothers. He likes his own way.' The 'shopping' money in her handbag was a perfect example.

Jasmine frowned.

'Of course, he's still a big improvement on my brothers,' Hallie added hastily. Mustn't forget she was supposed to be his wife. 'I don't feel nearly as trapped.' This was true. Probably because she knew she'd only agreed to the dutiful wife charade for a week.

'*I* feel trapped,' said Jasmine pensively. 'Sometimes all I can think about is finding a way out. When Nick first came to visit I saw him as an opportunity for escape. Of course, he's handsome and kind as well; a woman could do worse than be married to such a man… And you must understand, I didn't know he was already married.' Jasmine looked away, her face reddening. 'I tried to seduce him,' she said in a small voice. 'You should have seen his face. He was horrified.'

'Oh, Jasmine…' Hallie didn't know whether to applaud the younger girl's initiative or berate her for trying to sell her future so cheaply. 'There has to be another way.'

'There is,' said the younger girl. 'At least I think there is. Kai wishes to visit his family on the Mainland after the New Year. He's thinking of returning there permanently. If he goes I will try to persuade my father not to replace him.'

'That could work.'

Jasmine nodded. 'Hopefully it will make everyone happier, including Kai. He's been so irritable lately. And *moody*. And critical! He's driving me crazy.'

'Sounds like he's got woman trouble,' said Hallie. She had four big brothers; she knew the symptoms well.

'No,' said Jasmine with a firm shake of her head. 'I would know if there was a woman. He hasn't had a woman in his life for years.'

'No women at all? He's not…?'

'No!' said Jasmine indignantly. 'Definitely not! He's just…discerning.'

'I guess he can afford to be,' said Hallie, watching the younger girl closely. 'He's very handsome, don't you think? Almost as handsome as Nick.'

Jasmine's lips tightened. 'I guess,' she said, offhand.

'And he does the strong, silent thing very well.'

'If you like that kind of thing.'

'Many women do,' she assured the younger girl and smiled outright when Jasmine's eyes narrowed. Jasmine seemed to be harbouring a few protective instincts of her own when it came to Kai. 'How long did you say he's been moody for?'

'More than a year now,' said Jasmine glumly.

'And how old are you?'

'I was nineteen three weeks ago.'

Ah. 'Now I'm really inclined to think he's having woman problems. Maybe he's pining for an *unavailable* woman.'

'There *is* no *woman*!' said Jasmine hotly.

'There's you,' said Hallie quietly. 'Maybe Kai has feelings for you and doesn't know what to do with them. Maybe that's why he's so moody and irritable and wants to return to the Mainland.'

Jasmine blinked. Then she went white.

'I'm sorry,' said Hallie hurriedly, cursing her wayward mouth. 'I didn't mean to upset you. It was just a thought. I've only been here two days, what do I know?'

'It would explain many things,' said Jasmine with a tiny shake of her head. 'Oh, Hallie, I've been so *mean* to him lately.'

'I think Kai can handle a little mean, don't you?' said Hallie, her gaze meeting Kai's as he reappeared at the bottom of the stairs and started towards them with that silent, ground-eating stride. He was a warrior this one, a warrior steeped in the old ways; she knew the breed. Honour-bound to protect his charge; he would be equally determined to resist his feelings for her.

Not that he had the slightest chance of doing that indefinitely, thought Hallie as Kai's hooded gaze connected with Jasmine's newly aware one. Particularly if Jasmine decided she had feelings for him.

Water always prevailed in the end, no matter how hard the rock. Everyone knew that.

Lunch was a feast of flavours and hugely entertaining. The food hall was large, the crowd was raucous and

Hallie loved it. Almost as much as she enjoyed the silent byplay between Kai and Jasmine. Kai seemed to sense Jasmine's disquiet and watched her closely. Jasmine watched *him* when he wasn't watching her.

When Hallie could eat no more, when she was full to bursting and couldn't contemplate another mouthful, they cleared their table and headed up the escalator to browse the shops on the next level. Collector's shops, Jasmine told her distractedly before excusing herself and hurrying down a side corridor towards the bathrooms.

Kai watched her go, his gaze not leaving her retreating form. Moments later he was striding after her, catching her by the arm and swinging her round to face him just as she reached the bathroom door in an unmistakable display of baffled masculinity.

Hallie grinned and left them to it, wandering over towards an odd little corner shop while she waited. It was hard to tell what it sold; the red velvet drapes in the display windows weren't giving away any clues. And then she saw it. A solitary Chinese funeral vase sitting on a pedestal. It was old, so very old, and almost luminous in its fragile beauty. It was absolutely breathtaking.

The stark black signwork on the entry door was in Chinese. Hallie had no idea what it said. But a glance through the door showed more funeral vases inside, some on pedestals, some behind glass, and she simply couldn't resist a closer look.

The mood inside the shop was a sombre reflection of the stock, the salesman young and immaculately presented in a tailored grey suit. He looked up, surprise and wariness crossing his face as she came further into the shop. Maybe he didn't speak English and was worried about how to approach her, thought Hallie. Or maybe he'd forgotten how to speak at all; that was a possibility too given the number of customers he probably saw in a day. She sent him a reassuring smile and turned to the vases on display. Many of them were old. They were all beautiful. But none was lovelier than the one in the window.

'Excuse me,' she said to the young salesman, who still hadn't spoken but was watching her closely nonetheless, 'but do you speak English?'

'Some,' he said with a slight smile.

Some was good. Some was definitely better than none, which was the exact extent of her Cantonese. 'May I have a closer look at the vase in the window?'

'Madam probably wishes to buy a different kind of vase,' said the young man with surprising firmness. 'There are many other vases for sale on the next shopping level.'

'I'll keep that in mind,' she said. 'Right now I'm more interested in *these* vases.'

'Madam *does* realize that these vases are not for flowers.'

'I know. They're funeral vases.'

'Indeed so. They house the ashes of our beloved deceased.'

Yes, they did. And the one in the front window was perfect for a certain pretend husband whose postcoital sensitivity was non-existent! Nick wanted a vase. She wanted his money gone. Definitely a win-win situation. 'Would I be able to take a closer look at the one in the window?'

'It's very expensive, Madam.'

'I suspected as much,' she said smoothly. Not exactly salesman of the year, this one. She waited. So did he.

Finally he moved to the window, retrieved the vase and placed it carefully on the counter in front of her. She wanted her magnifying glass, contented herself with examining the vase inside and out. Definitely a collector's item.

'No refunds,' he said. 'Madam has to be very sure.'

'I'm sure.' She'd found what she was looking for, the tiny mark of a renowned dynasty craftsman. She wondered if the salesman knew what he had. 'How much?'

He named a price that made her gasp. He knew.

But the value was still there. The vase was in immaculate condition. It was even functional. Besides, it appealed to her sense of humour. She looked up at the salesman and gave him a wicked smile. 'It's for my husband. He deserves it.'

This time the salesman smiled back. 'And your husband's name?' He whipped a Palm pilot from his pocket, far more co-operative now that he had the sale.

She gave him Nick's name, the Teys' address, and all the cash Nick had given her that morning and then some.

'Do you have a picture of your husband?'

It was a strange question, thought Hallie. And no, she didn't.

'No matter, we will take care of it.' The salesman handed her the receipt. 'When would you like the vase delivered?'

'Today?' Hallie figured they probably didn't pack dynasty vases to go.

'Not possible, Madam.' The salesman was shaking his head regretfully.

'Well, I definitely need it before the New Year. Can you do that?' she asked him anxiously.

'Certainly,' said the salesman. 'That we can do. We are not slow like some.' His smile was charmingly crooked. 'We are professionals.'

Nick returned to his room just on five-thirty that afternoon to find Hallie fast asleep on the bed, clothes on, shoes off, and pillows everywhere. You could tell a lot about a person by the way they slept, thought Nick. Those who slept curled and guarded were careful, guarded people. Those who slept tidily and peacefully could generally be counted on to be the same awake. It was the sprawlers you had to worry about, and Hallie Bennett was most definitely a sprawler. A Titian-haired dryad, who even in her sleep had the ability to charm him with her vulnerability even as she overwhelmed him with her fearlessness. It was a wicked combination. Apply it to lovemaking and it was deadly. No wonder a man couldn't think straight afterwards. No wonder he'd botched his retreat and thrown money at her not two minutes later. He'd hurt her. He knew he had. And deeply regretted doing so.

Turning away, he loosened his tie and the top button of his shirt, saw the jug of water on the sideboard and poured himself a glass. He didn't need this. Didn't need Hallie dominating his thoughts in the middle of complex negotiations so that instead of thinking profit margins he was thinking of ways to apologize and put the warmth back in her eyes and in her smile when she looked at him.

Not that he'd come up with a solution that didn't leave him exposed and vulnerable, which meant that he hadn't come up with a solution at all.

'Hey,' said a sleepy voice from the bed. 'How's business?'

Nick turned to face her warily. 'Fast.' He was expecting coolness from her, didn't find it, so he told her more. 'John wants negotiations settled by Chinese New Year. Apparently if they drag on too long it could signal the start of an inauspicious year and we wouldn't want that.'

'Absolutely not.' Hallie smiled and sat up on the edge of the bed looking tousled and inviting. 'Is it doable?'

'John has a team working on it. From his perspective it is. From my side of things there's just me and an inch of fine print in two languages to wade through, and that's *after* we finalize the conditions.' She looked concerned, then thoughtful. He hadn't meant to tell her that much, didn't know why he had other than that she was a good listener when she wanted to be. 'It's doable,' he said with a shrug. 'How was your day?'

'Fun,' she said with a smile. 'I got your vase. It's being delivered. We also went sightseeing and did a great deal of eating. Oh, and I have something to tell you about Jasmine too. She only tried to seduce you because she saw you as an escape route from her father's over-protectiveness. I don't think we have to worry about her broken heart.'

Great, just great, all this subterfuge for nothing. Women! Nick scowled. Here he'd been trying to protect Jasmine from heartbreak and she'd been trying to *use* him.

'What?' said Hallie. 'I thought you'd be pleased.'

'I am.' He was. But between Hallie's blithe acceptance of his no-more-sex rule and Jasmine's ulterior motive for trying to seduce him, he was beginning to feel thoroughly under-appreciated. 'John's invited us out to dinner this evening,' he said by way of changing the subject before his ego was battered beyond repair.

'What time?'

'Seven.'

She glanced at the clock on the sideboard. 'Excellent. Enough time for a catnap. A person could really get used to this afternoon dozing caper.' She snagged a pillow and lay back down haphazardly. Her eyes drifted closed.

Nick couldn't move, wouldn't, for fear his feet would take him towards the bed and all this morning's rule-making would be for nothing. 'How are you feeling?' he asked huskily and cursed himself the moment the words left his lips. He knew what that question was about, knew exactly where it was heading. He wanted to know if she was physically able to take him again.

She came up onto one elbow in a single, fluid movement and fixed him with those glorious golden eyes. 'Are we talking mentally or physically?'

'Both.'

But Nick's dark, searing gaze slid from her face to her breasts and Hallie just knew what lay behind his question. 'You *want* me,' she breathed. 'You want to make love to me again!'

'No, I don't!'

Oh, yes, he did! And the knowledge that he did was downright empowering. She smiled slowly, arched back so that the thin silk of her shirt stretched taut across her breasts and had the satisfaction of seeing him pale.

'Stop that,' he ordered.

Her smile widened. 'You're absolutely right. Mustn't forget the rules.' She slid from the bed and sashayed towards the window with newfound confidence. 'You think anyone behind those windows over there in the distance would have a pair of binoculars?' she said. 'Because I thought I saw a glint of sunlight off something.'

'I didn't see anything,' he said.

That was because he'd been too busy watching her. 'Could have been a telescope, I guess. Or a camera.' She turned slowly, every move a subtle challenge. 'That's the trouble with a city this size. There's always someone watching.'

'We do *not* have an audience,' he said firmly.

'That you know of,' she corrected with a wicked grin. 'Better close the curtains just in case. Because if there was someone over there watching, they'd have an awfully good view of the bed.' Nick glanced at the bed at her words and Hallie thought she heard him mutter something beneath his breath. It didn't sound like a curse. Maybe he was praying.

'I'm going to shower before dinner,' he said doggedly. 'And I'm taking my clothes in with me.'

What, no parading that glorious body of his around in a towel? Spoilsport. 'Go.' Hallie waved him away. 'I've already showered. All I have to do is change clothes and I'm ready for dinner. I'll do it while you're in the bathroom. And I'll cut you a break and head on out to the terrace after that. Wouldn't want you breaking any more rules.' She tried hard not to smirk as he collected up fresh clothes and disappeared into the bathroom, closing the door behind him with far more force than was strictly necessary.

He wanted her. Nick Cooper, womanizer extraordinaire, wanted her, no matter what he'd said this morning. And, heaven help them both, she wanted him.

With distance came rational thought. Hallie stood on the terrace and looked out over the immaculately groomed gardens, then up at the clouds gathering in the sky, and thought about the situation sensibly. The heady recklessness that had come with the knowledge that Nick wanted her had settled and reality had swooped down on her like a cloak. Nick didn't *want* to want her. He couldn't afford the distraction; he'd told her that from the start. Hence their deal, their rules, and the ten thousand pounds he was paying her when the week was up. He was counting on her to stick to her side of the bargain.

As for her wanting him, well, that was only to be expected. It was an automatic response to a man like Nick, like breathing. It didn't necessarily mean she wanted a relationship with him. She'd fought hard for her independence from her well-meaning brothers;

fought dirty at times to keep it. She couldn't give it up. Wouldn't. She didn't want to be a cosseted corporate wife. Not even for Nick.

So it was settled. Nick was right. From now on she would stick to the plan. And to the rules. For both their sakes.

Nick joined her slightly before seven, freshly showered, shaven, and thoroughly eye-catching in dark trousers and yet another one of those crisp white shirts he wore without a tie. Honestly, how a woman was supposed to keep her resolve around such a man was anyone's guess.

Still, her smile of greeting was warm but not provocative, her body language welcoming but not enticing. 'I've had a rethink about the whole *wanting* dilemma,' she said casually, as if they were talking about nothing more important than the weather. 'I'm thinking denial is our best option.'

'I'm way ahead of you,' he said.

'I mean, it's only for a few more days, I'm sure it's doable. That way you get to concentrate on your work and I get the money to finish my diploma.'

'Exactly. Thanks, Hallie,' he said with a relieved smile.

'Don't smile,' she warned him. 'My resolve is not altogether reliable. I'm also thinking I should be more supportive. More corporate wife. What can I do?'

'Just what you have been doing. Keeping the conversation easy, finding common ground. In that regard you're doing fine.'

Uh, oh. A compliment. Dangerous ground. She hurried on. 'And I'm not sure where I should sit at dinner. Beside you? Opposite you? Where?'

'Beside me,' he said. 'John says the restaurant we're going to doesn't look like much but it has the best chilli crab in Hong Kong. I hope you like it hot and messy.'

She did. Hallie felt her mouth begin to water. Dinner didn't sound very corporate at all. It sounded like fun. She looked down at her black trousers and pink shirt. The trousers were fine. The shirt was a problem. Chilli crab juice splattered over pink silk was not a good look. 'Maybe I should change clothes.'

Or maybe she could try to be a tidy crab eater, she thought with a sigh as John, Jasmine and Kai joined them.

'I thought we might travel to the restaurant by ferry,' said John with a smile. 'Consider it an old man's indulgence. I delight in being out on the harbour at night.'

'He delights in showing our city off to visitors is what he really means,' whispered Jasmine to Hallie with a grin. 'But it's a journey you won't forget, I promise you. Shall we go?'

The ferry crossing was every bit as magical as Jasmine had promised, with Hong Kong Central on one shore and Kowloon on the other, each of them trying to outshine the other with their neon-draped skyscrapers and their laser displays that lit up the night. The harbour itself was vibrant with activity; the playful breeze and the gentle slap-slap of waves against the boat a sensual delight. But it was the skyline that truly dazzled her, the thousands upon millions of lights that turned the busy harbour into fairyland.

'You've made John's night,' said Nick. 'Just watching your face was enough.'

'Nick, it's so beautiful.'

'Yes, it is,' he said quietly. But he wasn't looking at the lights of Hong Kong. He was looking at her.

Disconcerted, Hallie clasped her arms around her waist and looked away.

'Cold?'

'No.'

But he pulled her closer anyway, so that his warmth was at her back and his arms were around her waist, and she let him because they had an audience.

Because it felt right.

The restaurant was nothing more than daytime pavement converted by plastic tables and chairs into a night-time eating area. Large bins of live crabs, their pincers tightly tied, lined one side of the makeshift square, bamboo growing in tubs lined another. The shopfront made the third side of the square. The fourth side was the gutter. It was badly lit, full of people, had no tablecloths whatsoever, and, more importantly, loads of paper napkins.

A ragged waiter hurried over to greet them and escorted them to a vacant table only to discover the tabletop sticky with beer. He skirted around it with an apologetic smile and showed them to an adjacent table. Bottled water arrived not thirty seconds later, along with cups for everyone. Chopsticks and crab-claw crushers appeared in front of each person. There was no menu. The restaurant served crab; that was all it served.

'Cooked any way you like,' the waiter assured them.

They ordered a chilli crab platter along with beer and white wine, and Hallie sat back to wait while her stomach growled and her mouth watered with every fragrant, steaming platter that emerged from the shop-front doorway.

'You're drooling,' said Nick. 'A good husband would point this out to his wife.'

'I am not drooling,' she said indignantly. 'I'm embracing the atmosphere.' As for him being a good husband… Ha! She wasn't even going to *start* thinking along those lines. As soon as this week was over she'd probably never see him again. She would do much better to think about *that*.

Another waiter emerged from the doorway, steaming crab platter in hand, and wove his way towards them, turning at the last minute to deliver the tray to the people who'd arrived just after them and been seated at the sticky table. 'Damn,' she muttered. 'So close and yet so far.'

'You're really not a half measures kind of girl, are you?' Nick was looking at her with a sort of wry resignation.

'Er, no. Is that a problem?'

'Not exactly.'

Hallie watched the activity at the next table as the waiter deftly served the topmost whole crab to a dark-haired European man and then distributed various bits and pieces of crab to his Asian companions.

'The first serving always goes to the honoured guest,' said Jasmine, noticing her preoccupation. 'It is the best.'

Hallie nodded. The Chinese were one of the most widespread and successful cultures on earth and force had nothing to do with it. Why use force when flattery and business acumen worked better? Only this time the flattery didn't seem to be working well at all. The dark-haired European was making strange choking noises and his face was turning an unnatural shade of purple. His hands were clutching at this throat; his eyes were glassy with tears.

'Just how hot *is* the chilli crab?' she whispered to Jasmine.

'Not that hot,' whispered Jasmine as the man toppled to the floor, foaming at the mouth, his chair sliding out from beneath him to ram into a half-full tub of crabs and knocking it over.

The rest was chaos.

Diners fled. Crabs scuttled beneath nearby tables, some with their pincers tied, some with them snapping. Nick was over by the fallen man and Kai with him. John Tey was barking what sounded like directions into his mobile phone and the crabs…the crabs were on the run.

'Feet up,' said John, and neither she nor Jasmine wasted any time arguing that it wasn't very ladylike. Jasmine leaned over and dangled her chopsticks in front of a crab and, when it bit, deftly lifted it up and shot it back into the tub.

'Don't do it again,' ordered her father.

Jasmine just smiled.

The kitchen staff descended; the apron-clad cook protesting loudly that this wasn't his doing, while nimble-fingered kitchen hands scooped escapee crabs into buckets.

By the time the paramedics arrived, the crowd around the fallen man was six deep. Hallie stood well out of the way as he was stretchered into an ambulance that zoomed off with its sirens wailing. He hadn't looked well. Truth be told, he'd looked practically dead.

'Probably just a reaction to seafood or something,' muttered Jasmine, worrying at her lower lip.

'Yeah,' said Hallie, reaching for Jasmine's hand and watching in silence as Kai casually liberated a piece of crab from the victim's plate, wrapped it in a napkin and pocketed it. He did the same for a crab claw from another plate. 'Reckon he's going to get them tested?'

'I think so,' said Jasmine, her attention all for Kai as he rejoined them.

'What?' he said, eying her warily.

'Go wash your hands.'

CHAPTER SIX

No ONE was hungry after that. Not for crab. John's suggestion that they return to the house and eat there met with instant approval although Jasmine looked a little panicked.

'Do we need to stop by a supermarket on the way home?' Hallie whispered as they headed for the wharf and the ferry terminal. Her brothers could strip a fully stocked kitchen of its food in less than two days; she knew what it was like to be asked to cook up a little gourmet something when the cupboard was practically bare.

'I have noodles,' whispered Jasmine. 'I can't feed guests *noodles*.'

'Of course you can,' countered Hallie. 'Nick loves noodles.' And if he didn't, he'd eat them anyway. 'May I help you prepare them?'

'My father will have a fit if you do,' said Jasmine.

'I'm taking that as a yes,' she said with a grin. 'Leave him to me.'

'Jasmine's going to give me a cooking lesson,' she told John cheerfully when they reached the house and he tried to usher them into the formal sitting room. 'She's going to show me how to cook stir-fry noodles. They're one of Nick's favourite dishes.'

Which was how they all came to be in the kitchen, every last one of them, with John fixing them drinks, Jasmine raiding the fridge for ingredients, and Kai setting a wok to heating and a huge pot of water to boiling on a gourmet gas stove.

'What are you up to now?' Nick asked her, pulling her aside when she would have headed over to help Jasmine.

'John's really embarrassed about the restaurant incident,' she whispered. 'I'm trying to avert disaster.'

'By eating in the man's kitchen? He's old school, Hallie. He probably thinks this *is* a disaster.'

'We're going to have a simple meal in simple surroundings and we're all going to enjoy it,' said Hallie firmly. And when he still looked uncertain, 'John Tey won't relax until you do. Trust me, it'll be fun.'

She was right decided Nick a few minutes later. The informality of the kitchen and the routine task of preparing food went a long way towards dispelling the sombre mood that had descended after they'd left the restaurant. It wasn't quite the way he envisioned a 'real' corporate wife would have handled the situation, but there was no denying that it worked. He watched Hallie quiz Kai about the type of oil he used and the paste he added, watched Kai chop ginger into slivers, his blade little more than a blur of speed. Watched Jasmine show similar skill with the cutting of bamboo shoots, wincing when Hallie immediately wanted to know how to speed chop too. He watched, with fatalis-

tic resignation, as Jasmine handed her the knife and
Hallie took her turn at the cutting board, albeit under
Kai's careful tutelage.

'So is this a traditional noodle recipe?' she wanted to know.

'Not quite,' said Jasmine, covering her grin with a
sip of white wine. 'This is a whatever-we-can-find-in-
the-fridge recipe. We make it a lot.'

Kai shot her an admonishing frown.

'Well, we do,' said Jasmine.

'So will I,' declared Hallie.

Kai just shook his head.

'Your wife is a lovely woman,' said John from
beside him. He too was watching the byplay. 'I'm glad
she could accompany you this time.'

Nick nodded awkwardly. He didn't like lying to the
older man about his marital status. He had John Tey's
measure now; the older man would have understood
the white lie he'd told to spare Jasmine's feelings. And
Jasmine, according to Hallie, wouldn't have been
heartbroken at all. All he would have had to do was
come clean with both of them and the problem would
have been solved. But it was too late to change the
play now, not without losing John's trust. He'd made
the call with the information available to him at the
time; he had to see it through.

'My daughter is often reserved around new
acquaintances, but not with Hallie,' observed John.
'Your wife has the knack of making others feel comfortable. She makes them smile from within. It is a
rare gift.'

Yes, it was. He just wished he were immune to it, that was all. Because he wasn't.

In what seemed like a remarkably short time, the vegetables were frying in the wok and noodles were bubbling away in a steaming pot of water. Hallie looked towards him, saw him watching her, and sent him a conspiratorial smile that warmed him through, before heading over to join them.

'Jasmine tells me you're fascinated by the Chinese Lion Dancing,' said John.

'Yes, we saw some boys practising their routines in the streets today.' Hallie grinned. 'I made Jasmine stay and watch until they'd finished. They were so young, the boys beneath the lion's head. And so skilful!'

'Lion dancing is often an honoured family tradition. The boys are taught by their father or their grandfather from a very young age,' said John. 'The current nationalal champions are performing at the Four Winds New Year's Eve Ball tomorrow evening. I've taken the liberty of acquiring tickets for us all if you're interested in attending.'

'I'm in,' said Hallie immediately, and with a somewhat belated glance in Nick's direction. 'That is, if Nick wants to go too.'

Nick nodded. It would take a stronger man than him to disappoint her.

'The ball is quite a spectacle,' said Jasmine as she set a heaped bowl of stir-fry in front of him, another in front of her father. 'There are fireworks at midnight and paper lanterns and decorations everywhere. Did you bring a gown?' she asked Hallie.

Hallie nodded. 'One. But it's kind of plain. Nick chose it and his mother agreed with him.' She sighed heavily. 'I was outnumbered.'

Plain, my ass, thought Nick. There was nothing plain about the way the floor-length gold sheath had clung to every delectable curve. Nothing ordinary about the way it made her skin glow and her eyes turn to amber.

'We could shop for another one tomorrow,' suggested Jasmine.

'No.' Hallie waved the suggestion aside. 'I was only teasing Nick. I love the gown. I'd have chosen it myself if I'd been given the chance. It may be plain, but the cut is superb.'

'You could accessorize,' he said, remembering the jewellery he'd borrowed from Stuart for just such an occasion. 'You could wear your necklace.'

'You mean the one I haven't even seen yet?' she replied archly. 'The one you chose without me? Maybe I could.' But her tone implied otherwise.

'I think you'll like it.'

Hallie sighed. 'I daresay I will, but that's not the point, is it? The point is I didn't get to help you choose it.'

Oh, yeah. Modern woman. Freedom. Equality. Respect. 'That was before I knew you liked to be in on the whole decision-making process,' he said by way of defence. 'I wanted to surprise you.'

'I think surprise gifts are wonderful,' said Jasmine. 'They're so romantic.'

'I think I agree,' said Hallie with a sigh. 'I may not be such a modern woman after all.'

'I don't know how you keep up,' murmured Kai as

he set another three bowls of noodles on the table and took a seat beside him.

'She sleeps a lot,' Nick countered dryly. 'That helps.'

Hallie was looking forward to getting some well-earned sleep. What she wasn't looking forward to was that pesky little time before she went to sleep. That five-metre walk from bathroom to bed, with her in her sleepwear and Nick over by the window all brooding and sexy. She made it to the bed by refusing to let her memories of this morning's lovemaking get the better of her. Did it by counting pillows. Denial was a hell of a lot easier when you didn't know what you were missing, thought Hallie glumly.

'I still have some work to do before tomorrow,' said Nick. 'It may be a while before I come to bed. I'll try not to disturb you.'

She risked a glance and immediately wished she hadn't as those knowing dark eyes met hers. 'It's okay,' she said, wiping damp palms down the sides of her boxers for girls. 'I have a plan.'

'You do?' His lips tilted. 'I can't wait to hear it.'

Actually it was more theory than plan. 'I think I need to sleep on the other side of the bed tonight.'

'You mean *my* side,' said Nick. 'And that would be because…?'

'It's obvious, isn't it? Last night I was trying to get to that side of the bed in my sleep, so I figure if I start there tonight I'll stay there.'

'That's it? That's your plan?'

She nodded.

'No pillows?'

She shook her head. Fat lot of good the pillows had done. 'I'm keeping it simple.'

'Let me get this straight. You want to sleep on my side of the bed tonight because that's what's going to stop you from wrapping yourself around me and—'

'Yes,' she interrupted hastily. 'That ought to do it.'

'What if it doesn't?' he asked silkily.

Good point. 'Well, maybe one person could sleep on top of the sheets and the other between them.' Yes, that could work. She hurried on. 'I'll sleep between the sheets and you can sleep on top of them. You slept without a sheet over you most of last night.'

'That's because I couldn't find it, not because I didn't want it.'

Oh. 'A gentleman would offer the sheets to the lady,' she said finally.

'Whatever happened to equality?' Nick's smile was pure rogue.

Hallie sighed heavily. It wasn't always easy, practising what you preached. 'Or we could toss a coin.'

Nick dug in his wallet for a coin and sent it spinning towards her. 'Tails and I get to sleep between the sheets,' he said.

It was tails.

'Fine.' Hallie lifted her chin. 'I'll stay on top of the sheets.'

Nick's smile deepened.

She lay down on the bed with her back to him and tried to block him out, tried to get her weary body to relax and sink into sleep, but it wouldn't comply. It was no good. She needed something over her. The red satin bedspread that she'd shoved to the bottom of the bed was her only option. She sat up, fully aware of Nick's amused eyes on her as she drew the coverlet over her and lay back down. There. Much better.

Ten minutes later she sighed heavily and shoved the cover aside. She was too hot beneath it. She sneaked another look at Nick. He wasn't working; rather, he was watching her. Laughing at her, to be more precise.

'Change of plans?' he enquired.

'Yes. Separation by sheet has been abandoned.' She crawled between the sheets defiantly, wrenching the top one into place so it covered her from chin to toe.

'I don't suppose you have a new plan?' he asked her.

'Er, no.' Nothing sprang to mind.

'We could always sleep top to tail,' he suggested. 'I could have my head up this end and you could have yours up there. That way if we moved towards one another through the night we'd end up next to feet.'

'No!' she said hastily. 'Absolutely not!' That would be bad, really bad, and it had nothing to do with feet. Because if he pulled the sheet *up* and she followed it *down* as she was wont to do, they'd end up next to something altogether different to feet and, dear Lord, she was getting all hot and bothered just *thinking* about what a man of Nick's obvious sexual experience might think to do in such a situation. Never mind keeping her own rampant curiosity under control.

She was still tender, still a little sore from this morning's lovemaking. What if Nick took it into his head to, you know, soothe her? She'd be lost. Possibly begging. Hell, she was close to begging already and she was only thinking about it. 'No top to tail.' She tried to make her voice sound firm, had the sneaking suspicion she'd just done a halfway decent Marilyn Monroe impersonation.

'Why not?' he said.

'Because I'm a lot shorter than you, that's why, and I might, ah, move *down* the bed somewhat. Especially if you're pulling the sheets that way. I might not end up next to feet at all.'

'You're right.' His eyes darkened. 'Top to tail is definitely out.' He didn't look amused any more, he looked...dangerous. 'I guess will-power will have to do.' He came over to her then, came right over to the bed and tucked the sheet firmly around her. 'Get some sleep,' he ordered, and leaned forward just enough to set his lips to hers for a kiss that would have been chaste but for the tip of his tongue that went skittering across her upper lip.

It was enough. More than enough given where her thoughts had been to have her gasping in helpless delight and clenching the sheets to keep her hands from reaching for him. But her body arched towards him anyway, ached for him, and Nick knew it did, dammit. And groaned for the both of them.

'Stop it,' he muttered. 'Stop me. We are *not* doing this. I have too much work to do.'

'Then go do it,' she whispered, closing her eyes tightly as if maybe, somehow, if she didn't see him he'd be easier to resist.

It was a long time before she fell asleep.

Even longer before Nick finally went to bed.

Hallie woke the following morning snuggled into Nick's side with her head on his shoulder and a hand at his waist. She lay perfectly still, her brain trying to figure the best way to extricate herself from his embrace while her body wondered why she would ever want to, her body being more than happy to stay right where it was. But that wasn't the point. The point was that she and Nick had decided lovemaking was out and it was going to take a joint effort to stick to that agreement. If either of them weakened they were both lost; it was as simple as that.

Hallie held her breath as she eased her hand from his waist and started to inch away from him, watching his face for any signs of waking, but he was sound asleep. There were shadows under his eyes that made him look vulnerable, shadows along his jaw that made him look dangerous. And a strength in his face that called to her even as she railed against it. What was it about this man that made him so hard to resist?

Because it wasn't his face and it wasn't his body, although both were gorgeous. No, it was something far more intrinsic than that, something that called to her very soul. And made it tremble. She backed up some more, felt the edge of the bed with her toes. Almost there. One foot on the floor and now the other as she eased her body from the mattress and stood up. Mission completed.

But she'd taken the sheet with her, which left her with a new problem. To cover Nick up again or not to cover. He didn't look cold. No goose-bumps on that gloriously sculpted chest. She made the mistake of letting her gaze travel down his body and swallowed hard at the substantial bulge beneath his boxers. Never mind if he was cold or not, *she* needed him covered up. She gathered up the sheet and was just about to float it over his body when some sixth sense made her glance up at his face.

He was awake, watching her through slitted eyes, with a smile on his face and an invitation in his eyes that was practically irresistible. 'Going somewhere?' he said.

Hallie dropped the sheet and took a hasty step backwards, almost falling over her feet in the process. 'I, ah, I thought I'd get up early and go down and see if Jasmine needs a hand with the New Year's Eve preparations.'

Nick's smile deepened. 'Good of you,' he said.

'Yes, well, things to do.' Hallie smiled brightly as her heart pounded and her skin tingled at the sound of his sleepy, sexy rumble. With one last wayward glance for the dazzling display of blatant masculinity spread out in front of her she fled to the bathroom before temptation and Nicholas Cooper's smile got the better of her.

With Nick and John at John's offices and Kai away arranging crab analysis, Hallie and Jasmine got down to the serious business of decorating the house for the forthcoming New Year. There were oranges to stack into small pyramids with incense on either side as offerings to the ancestors, beautiful red envelopes to stuff with crisp new money as gifts for friends and relatives, and exquisite paper lanterns to light up the terrace come nightfall. There was grain to offer the Rooster, for it was his year, and he must be made welcome. There were horoscopes to consult. Nails to paint a bright, bold red, and the services of a hairdresser to arrange for later in the day.

They left the dresses until last. Hallie's choice was simple, she would wear the gold gown. Jasmine had a far greater selection to choose from, but by lunchtime they'd narrowed it down to two. A full-length, midnight-blue satin gown with a demure front and next to no back, and a strapless burgundy gown with gold embroidered accents on the bodice. Both were gorgeous. Neither woman could choose between them.

Kai returned in time for lunch and seemed unusually quiet, even for him. When lunch was eaten, the dishes cleared away and the kitchen spotless, he spoke.

'May I speak with you in private?' he said to Jasmine.

'Is this about the crabmeat?' Jasmine eyed him curiously.

'No.'

Hallie watched them retreat to John's office with a nagging sense of foreboding; Kai looked like a man with a lot on his mind. He took off in the Mercedes not ten minutes later and Hallie found Jasmine in her room, standing by the window, her eyes wet with tears.

'He's leaving for the Mainland next week and he's not coming back,' said the younger girl shakily. She gave a tiny, helpless shrug. 'I really didn't think he'd go.'

'Oh, Jasmine…'

'I don't want him to go. I thought I did, but I

don't.' Fresh tears welled in the younger girl's eyes before she lowered her head, a silky curtain of hair covering her distress.

'I thought you felt trapped,' said Hallie gently. 'I thought you *wanted* your independence.'

'I want Kai.'

'Because he's always been there for you. Because he's safe.'

'No! Not just because of that.' And with a sob, 'I thought he loved me.'

No prizes for guessing who'd put that idea into her head, thought Hallie, and cursed herself for doing so. She'd been thinking about Jasmine and Kai and the situation they were in; thinking that some time apart would benefit them both. 'Think about it from Kai's perspective,' she urged the younger girl. 'Even if he does love you he's been your protector now for almost ten years. He knows full well it wouldn't be fair of him to burden you with his feelings. Not when you've had so little opportunity to discover who you are and what you want.'

'I know who I am,' said Jasmine with quiet certainty. 'And I want Kai.'

'Maybe you do. But wouldn't you rather come to him as an equal? As a woman he can love and respect rather than a girl he feels he needs to watch over?'

Jasmine was silent. Finally she lifted her head and turned to Hallie, uncertainty in her eyes this time, rather than desolation. 'Of course I would.'

'Then maybe this is for the best,' said Hallie softly. 'I for one think you're a very lucky woman. What more could you want than the love of a beautiful warrior who knows what you need and is willing to give it to you even if it means losing you? Don't you see?' Hallie tucked the hair that was clinging to Jasmine's tear stained cheek back behind her ear with gentle fingers. 'He's setting you free.'

Two hours later, after a shower for Jasmine and a cup of tea for them both, they were once again standing in front of the two dresses that hung from the doors of Jasmine's wardrobe.

'Give it a year,' said Jasmine thoughtfully.

'Or two.'

'I don't think I can wait that long.'

'I didn't say you couldn't see him at all,' said Hallie. 'And I definitely didn't say you shouldn't give him something to remember you by. Is he coming to the ball?'

'I don't know,' said Jasmine. 'There's a ticket for him.'

'I'm thinking the blue dress. The front is demure, it's what Kai expects, but then when you turn around and he sees all that skin…bam! How were you thinking of wearing your hair?'

'Up,' said Jasmine.

'Perfect. What about jewellery?'

Jasmine went over to a small wooden jewellery box and lifted out a long silver chain so fine you could hardly see the links. There was a single teardrop pearl a shade lighter than the colour of her skin dangling from it. 'I thought this. It's not expensive, more of a trinket really, but it was my mother's. There's no clasp; it slips over the head. But it's too long.'

'Not if you wear it backwards,' said Hallie.

'Oh,' said Jasmine. 'Now *I'm* thinking the blue dress. And I shall ask Kai to dance with me. It's a ball; people do dance with one another at balls.'

Nothing wrong with the younger girl's feminine instincts, thought Hallie, and nodded enthusiastically. 'A slow dance,' she said. 'A waltz, so he has to put his arm around you and touch all that skin.'

Jasmine smiled slowly.

Hallie smiled back. Kai was toast.

Nick and John returned earlier than expected around mid-afternoon.

'We're almost there,' said Nick when Hallie dragged him into the garden to get the low-down. 'John has his lawyers working on the documents now. I've faxed them through to mine, but I can't see any problems. All we have to do is sign them.'

'And you're happy with the deal?' she asked him.

'It's a little less than I was hoping for in some respects, a little more in others. I think John feels the same way.' Nick shot her a weary smile. 'I have a new appreciation for haggling as an art form, but in the end we got there. It's a fair deal. We both stand to make a lot of money.'

'So tonight we celebrate.' Hallie looked at him in concern. He didn't look as if he felt like celebrating. He looked exhausted. 'Are you going to make it through to midnight? Why don't you go upstairs and rest for a while? Take a nap.'

'I would, but the bed upstairs holds a few too many

memories of you in it. I won't rest if I go up there and I sure as hell won't sleep.'

'Are you flirting with me?'

'Nope.' He eyed her darkly, a man too tired and tense to bother with the niceties. He needed rest, needed to sleep, but if that wasn't an option the next best thing he could do was take a break. From his work, from the strain of pretending to be married to her, and from the Teys, nice as they were.

'Come into the city with me, then. I have to find a New Year's gift for Jasmine. It'll do you good. Do us both good.'

'How do you figure that?' he asked.

'I want to relax and be myself for a while. Not Hallie Cooper, corporate wife. Not Hallie Bennett, partner in lies. I just want to be me. I want you to be you.'

'Time Out,' said Nick.

Exactly. Trust a man to use a sports metaphor to describe a burgeoning identity crisis, but whatever worked. 'So what do you say?'

Twenty minutes later they were standing on a chaotic sidewalk in downtown Hong Kong, Kai having dropped them off and Nick having assured him that they'd catch a taxi back. He was tired, he was irritable, and denying his fierce sexual attraction to Hallie really wasn't working for him, but there was no denying her suggestion they take a break was a good one. 'Do you have anything particular in mind as a gift for Jasmine?' he asked her.

'I'm sure I'll know it when I see it,' she said blithely.

Nick groaned. This was bad. This was going to take for ever.

'I am open to suggestions,' she added.

There was a god.

'Perfume,' he said firmly, not two minutes later as they stood at a department-store perfume counter. 'We'll get her some perfume.'

'Predictable,' said Hallie with a sigh.

'Reliable,' he corrected, and, staring at the dazzling selection of perfumes on offer, 'You choose.'

'I'll have to smell them first and find the one that fits Jasmine best. Of course, I already know what half of them smell like so it shouldn't take too long.'

Maybe perfume hadn't been such a fast and easy solution to the gift-buying problem after all, thought Nick gloomily as Hallie picked up a nearby tester bottle and sniffed.

'This one's too overpowering. Jasmine's far more delicate than that,' she said with a grimace, hastily returning the bottle to the counter and picking up another. 'And this one's too old-fashioned.' She moved along the counter to the next cluster of little glass bottles, plucked one from the middle and handed it to him. 'Try this one.'

He took it, sniffed it. 'Nice.' But Hallie rejected it.

'It is nice, but it's all top note, there's no depth. It's too chaste. Jasmine's a woman, not a girl.'

'Maybe she could wear it in one of her more girlish moments,' he suggested, and stifled a sigh at Hallie's measured, 'No.' This was going to take for ever.

The next one was nice too. Hell, they were all nice,

but according to Hallie they just weren't right. And then Hallie pointed towards a small vial high on a shelf and the salesgirl obligingly got it down for her. She lifted the stopper, took a deep sniff of the perfume and sighed happily. 'This is it,' she said. 'This is Jasmine.'

Nick took it and smelled it. Nice. Why it was Jasmine and the others weren't was beyond him, but if Hallie was satisfied, so was he. 'I see what you mean,' he said, with a nod for good measure.

'Liar!' Her laughter was warm and spontaneous, a reflection of the woman. 'Tell me why I chose it.'

'Er, whim?' Her eyes narrowed and her chin came up. He still loved that look.

'I've just given you some huge hints on how to buy perfume for a woman. Huge! You could have at least paid attention.'

'I did pay attention.'

'Alrighty, then.' Her hands went to her hips. 'Choose one for me.'

Nick stared at Hallie, stared at the perfumes, all two hundred odd bottles of the stuff, and nearly broke out in a cold sweat. 'I could use a hint,' he said.

Hallie moved down the counter again, to yet another cluster of bottles, her hand hovering over one particular bottle before finally picking it up. 'Here. This is one my mother used to wear; it brings back some wonderful memories of her. It's warm, elegant, beautiful. I love it, but I don't wear it.'

'You call that a hint?'

'Big one.' Her voice was grave, but her eyes were laughing.

Nick sighed heavily, took the perfume her mother used to wear out of her hand and sniffed. He knew that smell, loved its memories because Clea wore it too. It wasn't Hallie; she was right. But it was close.

He attacked the problem systematically, working his way through the entire cluster of perfumes in front of him and rejecting all but three bottles. He took his time with these, undecided, before making his final choice and handing it to her. 'This one.'

'Are you sure?' she teased. 'How do you know? Because I swear your nose went on strike ten bottles ago.'

'Smell it,' he urged.

She took a deep sniff. It had some of the same ingredients as her mother's perfume, the same warmth in the base, but it was different too. More exotic and youthful. More vibrant.

'Well?' he asked gruffly.

'I like it.'

'How much do you like it?'

'A lot.'

Nick's relieved smile was boyishly endearing and Hallie felt her heart stutter. He was a curious mixture, Nicholas Cooper. Smooth as silk one minute, as sweet as Friday's child the next. 'Promise me you'll wear it for me tonight,' he murmured.

Yep, just as smooth as silk. 'Now I'm going to choose one for you,' she told him.

'Don't!' he said, clearly horrified by the notion. 'Walk with me through the alleyways for half an hour. That's all I want. Let me show you the Hong Kong I like best.'

She could do that.

She loved doing just that, because it was here that she found what had been missing in the spotless airport and glittering department stores; here she found the hawker stalls and the food carts; the scent of yesteryear and the bustle of an exotic, vibrant culture.

This was the Hong Kong Nick liked best? She should have guessed. Nick would always seek out the real, add a dash of what if and colour it magical. It was part of his charm.

What kind of woman would he choose when he finally *did* take a wife? Hallie wondered. Would she laugh with him and delight in the boy beneath the man? Would she be worldly and elegant? An asset to his business interests? Would he choose a *real* corporate wife? Hallie was so preoccupied with her thoughts she almost fell over Nick as he knelt down to examine a tiny street urchin's meagre fake watch selection that had been lined up with military precision on a dirty scrap of towel.

'Cartier,' he said, grinning up at her. 'Bargain. You want one?'

Dammit, she knew this would happen. She was falling for him. 'That one,' she said, pointing towards a plain-faced gold watch in the middle of the row. 'Does it work?'

'The hands are moving. That's always a good sign,' he said as he handed over enough money to buy ten fake watches and waved away the change. 'Where to now?' he said, handing her the watch.

'Back to the Teys' if this watch is correct. I have

to be back by five-thirty if I want the hairdresser to style my hair.'

'And do you?'

'Absolutely. I'm off to a ball in a designer gown and there'll be dancing and music and a countdown to mid-night. I want the works. Tonight I'm going to feel like Cinderella.'

'Does that mean I have to be your Prince Charming?'

'You can *try* to be my Prince Charming,' she countered with a smile. They were standing beside a busy road and a taxi was heading their way in the centre lane. Nick saw it about the same as time she did and stepped to the side of the pavement and raised his hand. The taxi swerved abruptly and shoehorned itself into the side lane to the accompaniment of blaring horns and rude gestures.

'I think he's seen us,' said Nick.

'Yeah, but do we want to get in a car with him?' she muttered. The taxi wasn't slowing down. If anything it was speeding up. 'He's not stopping,' she said and stepped back from the kerb just as someone stumbled into Nick from behind, pushing him onto the road.

'Nick!'

It all happened in a screaming blur. She lunged for his shirt, caught the very edge of it and heaved him backwards with all her strength as the taxi sped past, mere millimetres from the guttering. There was nothing to break her fall as they tumbled back in a heap, her elbow connecting painfully with the cement, her head hitting it moments later, followed by Nick's big body pushing every last ounce of breath from her body as he landed on top of her. Then he was on his hands and knees beside her and she was seeing double, triple even. Either that or the entire population of Hong Kong was staring down at her.

'Hallie. Hallie! Can you hear me?'

Nick's face loomed above her, a familiar face against a sea of oriental ones, and she clung to it as a shipwrecked sailor clung to a beacon. 'He wasn't going to stop,' she whispered.

'No. He wasn't.' Nick looked almost as shaken as she felt as his hands carefully brushed a stray strand of hair from her eyes. 'How do you feel? Where do you hurt?'

'I scraped my elbow,' she said. 'I hit my head.'

'How many fingers am I holding up?'

'None. Your hands are in my hair.'

'Right,' said Nick. 'How many now?'

'Two.' Her head was starting to clear, her vision was returning. She tried to sit up, and was immediately assisted by a hundred helpful hands that didn't stop at sitting but lifted her gently to her feet. 'Thank you,' she said, and, 'Thank you, again,' as someone handed her her handbag and the bag with the perfumes in it. There was an animated discussion going on somewhere in the crowd, lots of shouting and hand-waving. Finally a business-suited Chinese man approached them both.

'You were pushed,' he told Nick. 'This man says he saw it.' He pointed to a wizened little man at the back of the crowd. 'He says it was a man wearing a red cap, zip jacket, and jeans. A young man.'

Nick nodded, thanked both men.

'I thought I saw someone push you too,' said Hallie, 'but I didn't see a face.' She'd been too busy trying to grab him.

'C'mon.' He was leading her towards a quiet doorway of a shop that had already closed for the evening. 'I think we should get you to the hospital. Get you checked out.'

'No, Nick! That'll take hours!' They'd miss the ball. 'I fell over and you landed on top of me, that's all. I grew up playing football with my brothers, I'm used to it.' Okay, so she was exaggerating. Just a little. He didn't look as if he was buying it anyway. He lifted her arm for a closer look at her elbow; she turned her arm so she could see it herself. It was a nasty graze. Damn. Hallie scowled. 'This is so not going to go with my gown.'

'Be serious,' he said gruffly. 'You could have concussion.' He threaded his hands through her hair and tilted her head forward, examining her skull with gentle fingers.

'Ow!' She winced when he hit the spot that had connected with the concrete.

'It's swelling,' he told her. 'You're going to have an egg.'

'I'm also going to have the services of a hairdresser. You'll never know it's there. Really, Nick. I'm okay.'

His eyes were dark and searching as his hands moved from her hair to frame her face. 'You scared me,' he said simply. And lowered his lips to hers.

He was very gentle, very careful, and Hallie trembled at the tenderness she found in his embrace. She closed her eyes, lifted her hands to his shoulders, and

opened her mouth to him, revelling in his warmth and
the dark, delicious taste of him. He took his time, such
an agonizingly long time he took before his tongue
touched hers and duelled. There was no rush, no haste
and he built that kiss so slowly and surely that stars
exploded in her head for the second time that afternoon. *Here* was what she'd been waiting for all her
life. Passion laced with sweetness. Strength tempered
by caring, and she wound her arms around his neck
and drank in that sweetness and that strength with no
thought for anything but the aching need to have it.

It was Nick who broke the kiss, his breathing ragged
as he rested his forehead against hers. 'We have an
audience,' he muttered. 'And we're in a public place.
The way I figure it, we're still within the rules here.'

'Lucky us,' she whispered. It didn't feel as if they
were still working within the rules. It felt as if they
were breaking every last one of them.

He stepped back, seemingly reluctant to let her go.
'Do you want to see a doctor?'

It was a question, not an order, and drove home the
point that for all the similarities between Nick and her
brothers, in this he was quite, quite different. Seeing a
doctor was her call, her choice to make and she made
it. 'I'm fine,' she said firmly. 'Just fine.'

'C'mon.' Nick didn't know whether to curse her stub-
bornness or applaud her spirit. 'Let's get you home.'

CHAPTER SEVEN

'WHAT happened?' cried Jasmine when she opened the front door to them, sweeping them through to the sitting room and settling Hallie into the nearest chair. 'Stay there,' she ordered and disappeared at a run. When she returned she had Kai and a first-aid kit with her and Nick almost sighed his relief as Jasmine fished cloth and antiseptic from the kit and set to work on Hallie's elbow. She'd scared him half to death when he'd seen her lying there on the pavement looking so small and broken and only half conscious, and her decision not to consult a doctor didn't sit well with him. 'She hit her head as well,' he told Jasmine.

Jasmine's gaze flew to Hallie's eyes. 'We need a torch,' she said firmly. 'We need to check her pupils for dilation.'

'I'm not concussed,' protested Hallie. 'I'm fine.'

'Don't argue,' he said. 'Just let her check.' And with a wry smile, 'For my sake if not for yours.'

'You *are* as bad as my brothers,' she grumbled.

'Yeah, but my delivery's far better.'

'What happened?' Kai asked him quietly.

'I was trying to hail a taxi and stood a little too close to the kerb. Hallie pulled me back and we fell.'

'You were pushed,' said Hallie, and to Kai, 'Someone pushed him off the kerb and into the path of an oncoming taxi. I only saw a big jacket and a cap but there was an old man there who saw his face. He said it was a young man and that he did it deliberately.'

'You were pushed?' asked Kai.

'Someone stumbled into me,' he countered. 'I don't know that it was deliberate.'

Hallie stared at him defiantly. 'If it was an accident, why didn't he stick around to make sure you were all right?'

'Maybe he was too scared to.'

'Did you get the old man's name?' asked Kai.

'I didn't think it was necessary,' said Nick. 'Why?'

'I checked on the sick diner from the restaurant. He's in a coma. The doctors suspect some kind of poison. I took the crabmeat to a private lab for testing, but so far the tests have been inconclusive. If it does contain poison it's a rare one.' Kai paused. 'There is another disturbing fact about last night's incident,' he said quietly. 'The platter was not meant for that particular party. It was meant for us. And if it is as I suspect and only the topmost portion of crab was poisoned, that means it was meant for you.'

'What? You're saying someone's trying to kill me?' Whatever direction he thought Kai's conversation was going to go, this wasn't it. 'Are you serious?'

'I'm always serious,' said Kai. And with his next

breath, 'Let me know if you still wish to attend the ball tonight and I'll arrange extra security.'

Nick had taken the news that someone could be trying to kill him surprisingly well, thought Hallie as she watched him pace their guest room not ten minutes later. 'Do you have any idea who would want to kill you?' she said thoughtfully.

'No.'

'Maybe it's someone who doesn't want you going into partnership with John. Maybe they've invented a game just like yours and will lose everything if they don't stop your product from hitting the market.'

'Hallie…' he began warningly.

'Or a resentful distributor who failed to get your business,' she said. 'How many did you reject before you decided to go with the Tey Corporation?'

Nick rolled his eyes. 'A few, but I really don't think—

'Or a woman scorned. There's a thought. I bet there are plenty of those.'

'I do not scorn,' he snapped. 'I just…'

'Leave?'

'Yeah, and, since we're on the subject, I'm terminating your contract. I'm sending you home.'

'Oh?' She was prepared to be calm, at least for now. 'And why is that?'

'I don't want you involved in this. I want you back home and safely out of the way.'

Now he was definitely starting to sound like her brothers. And she'd had such high hopes for him too. 'What happened to *we're in this together as equals*?'

'It stopped when I found out someone was trying to kill me. You didn't sign on for this, Hallie. I don't want you involved.'

'I want to stay and help,' she said stubbornly.

'No,' he said, equally stubborn. 'You can't help with this.'

'I did today.'

'And look what it got you! A busted elbow and a concussion headache!'

'I do not have a concussion headache,' she said indignantly. 'It's just a normal one.'

'Look...' His expression softened. 'You saved my life today; don't think I don't appreciate it, but I don't want you getting hurt again. Not because of me.'

'Fine,' she said, waving him towards the telephone. 'Book the plane seat.'

Five minutes later he slammed the phone down in frustration. 'You knew there wouldn't be any seats available,' he said accusingly.

'Of course I knew. It's Chinese New Year. Everyone's travelling to visit their families. I'm betting you couldn't get plane tickets back to the UK any earlier than the ones we've already got.' Nick's scowl told her she was right. 'Cheer up, Nick. It's not that bad. You're the one they want dead, not me. And they only *might* want you dead. We're not exactly sure about that yet. I'm probably not in any danger at all.'

'If I had any sense I'd call one of your brothers to come and get you.'

'Well, you could,' she said doubtfully. 'But then you really *would* be a dead man.' She glanced at her watch and groaned. 'What are we going to do about this ball? Do you still want to go? Because if you do, we're going to have to start getting ready.'

'Do you?'

Hallie shrugged. She did want to attend the ball. Badly. But not if it was going to put Nick in danger. This one was *his* call.

'We're probably jumping to conclusions about someone trying to kill me,' he said at last.

'This is true.'

'Kai did say he'd arrange extra security.'

Also true.

'And I'll be damned if I'll stop living before I'm dead!'

She liked his attitude, she really did. 'So we're going?'

'Yeah,' said Nick. 'We're going.'

Hallie showered quickly, shrugged on a borrowed robe and slipped down to Jasmine's room to get her hair done and give her the perfume. When she returned she found Nick already dressed for the ball, a handsome heartbreaker in an elegant black dinner suit that looked tailormade for him and probably was. She should have been more immune to his looks by now, desperately wanted to be, but there was something about the combination of dark hair, dark suit, and a snowy white shirt that made her breath catch in her throat. And then he spoke.

'Shouldn't you be getting ready?' he said.

And the spell was broken. 'Keep talking,' she ordered, scooping her gown from the closet on the way through to the bathroom. 'I'll be ready before you've finished your spiel about how bad mannered it would be to be late. Which we won't be.' She left the bathroom door ajar as she slipped her robe off and slid the dress over her head—all the better to hear Nick's disgruntled mutterings by, and he didn't disappoint.

'You've got five minutes,' he warned, but she was already up to make-up and she only needed two. Shoes next, dainty stilettos that added a good couple of inches to her height. Next a dab of the perfume Nick had given her at her pulse points and finally her wrap, amber-coloured silk a couple of shades lighter than her gown, and she was done.

One minute remaining. Time to see if Nick approved of the way the corporate wife was packaged. She entered the bedroom regally, only to find him staring out the window, trying hard to exude manly patience. 'I'm ready,' she said.

He turned, studied her from head to toe, and the purely masculine appreciation in his eyes was immensely gratifying. 'You're beautiful,' he murmured. 'But you're not ready.'

'I'm not?'

'You forgot your jewellery.'

She had her rings on, didn't she? Yep. Hard to miss them. 'I really hope you're not talking about the watch you bought me today.'

Nick pointed towards a grey velvet case on the counter.

'Oh. You mean *that* jewellery.' The jewellery she'd

never seen. The jewellery he'd chosen without her. 'I forgot about it.'

'You *forgot* about it?' Nick appeared disbelieving.

'Maybe if I'd *seen* it I wouldn't have,' she told him sweetly.

'You can see it now.'

Hallie walked over to the counter and her hands came up, seemingly of their own volition, to stroke the long velvet box, but then she hesitated.

'What *now?*' said Nick.

'I've seen the necklace Jasmine's wearing tonight and it's very simple,' she said with a frown. 'I wouldn't want to go overboard in comparison.'

'Maybe this is simple too,' said Nick. 'Why don't you open it and see?'

Why didn't she? She was nearly bursting with curiosity, wondering what he'd chosen and whether she'd like it. Worried that she wouldn't. More worried that she would. There was only one way to find out. Hallie opened the box with careful hands. And gasped.

The necklace was like a pearl choker in design, but where the pearls would have been there were diamonds, big carat-sized diamonds that glittered brilliantly in the light. As far as jewellery went it was exquisite, eye-popping even, because Hallie was pretty sure hers were halfway out of her head. But it wasn't simple.

'Do you like it?' he asked.

'Are you serious? It's absolutely gorgeous.' He was taking it from the box, and putting it around her neck, his fingers warm and gentle against her skin as he fastened the clasp.

'It suits you. I knew it would.' He steered her towards the bathroom. 'Go take a look in the mirror.'

Hallie went and looked, made a minute adjustment to its position. There, now it was perfect and now she was thinking Audrey Hepburn in *Breakfast at Tiffany's* or Grace Kelly in anything, both of them as redheads, of course.

'What do you think?' said Nick from the doorway. He was leaning lazily against it, his smile indulgent and his eyes dark.

'It probably wouldn't do to bring it all this way and not wear it,' she said, while the diamonds around her neck blazed with every movement she made. They probably wouldn't overshadow Jasmine's teardrop pearl all that much, she decided, a touch desperately. The diamonds were stunning in a different way, that was all. They might even *complement* Jasmine's pearl.

'There are earrings to match.'

'Oh, well…' May as well do things properly. A minute later she was wearing them too. 'Do you think it's too much?'

'You could always take the dress off,' he muttered. 'That'd work.'

'Focus,' she said sternly. 'You're losing sight of the rules.'

'You don't say.'

'You can look all you like,' she said generously. 'You even get to touch providing we're in a public place and have an audience. You just don't get to take at the end of the evening. It'll be character building.'

And with a final sweep of the bedroom for the silk purse that matched the wrap, she headed for the door.

The ballroom at the Four Winds hotel was where British Colonialism met Asian Affluence and a spectacle of such unbridled opulence that it left Hallie gaping. There were champagne-glass pyramids complete with nervous waiters, elaborately costumed opera singers with faces whiter than snow. There were five-tier chandeliers and peacock feathers by the bucketful. There was a dance band over by the dance floor, and there were Hong Kong's finest—dressed in their finest—mingling graciously.

'How on earth am I supposed to go back to selling shoes after this?' she murmured, desperately trying to commit it all to memory: the colours and textures, the scents and the sounds.

'Maybe you won't have to,' murmured Nick and Hallie felt her heart skip a beat.

'You'll have enough money after this to get through your diploma without selling more shoes, won't you?' he added.

Oh. *That* was what he meant. For a minute there, she'd thought that Nick had fallen in love with her, and for a moment she'd wondered what it would be like to be Mrs Nicholas Cooper for real. For a moment there, she'd thought it would be just fine. But that was ridiculous. The whole point of agreeing to this charade in the first place was so she could focus on her real dream, the one that didn't involve Nicholas Cooper and fairy-tale endings. The one that involved hard work, independence and the satisfaction that came with achieving one's goals. 'I'll make it enough,' she said firmly. 'You're right, selling shoes is over. Asian Art World, here I come. Here's to you for helping to make it happen.'

'I've watched you, Hallie.' There was a serious note in his voice. 'I've seen the enthusiasm and the energy you bring to everything you do and I know without a doubt that when you do decide on a career, be it in the art world or somewhere else, you're going to be a huge success. Don't ever doubt it.'

'Thank you,' she said quietly. For all his faults, and, yes, not falling helplessly in love with her was one of them, Nicholas Cooper believed in her. Hallie felt her heart falter, felt it stumble before righting itself, and when it did it wasn't altogether hers any more. Some of it was Nick's. Not that she was inclined to let him know that.

So she pinned on a smile, a smile that became more genuine as she was introduced to friends and acquaintances of John and of Jasmine. She nodded to husbands and mingled with wives as they ogled the diamonds around her neck overtly, Nick covertly, and made laughing conversation with her.

Partnering Nick to a ball was easy. He was gorgeous, charming, and knew exactly when to leave her to her own devices and when to stay by her side. 'You're a very good escort, you know that, don't you?' she said as he whisked her half-finished glass of champagne from her hand, handed it to a passing waiter, and snagged a cool glass of water as a replacement. It was exactly what she wanted. 'How did you know I wanted water?'

'I didn't,' said Nick. 'But you hadn't touched your champagne in over an hour and it's getting warm in here so I figured it was worth a shot.'

'Gorgeous, generous *and* attentive,' said Hallie dryly. 'Is there anything you're not good at?'

'Rules,' he said, his eyes darkening. 'I'm not real good with rules. Dance with me.'

Hallie took a quick sip of her water, felt it slide, wet and cool, down her suddenly dry throat. 'I'm not sure dancing's a good idea for us.' Dancing meant touching, touching meant wanting, and when touching, wanting and Nick came together she was inclined to forget the rules herself. 'I'm thinking we should forgo the dancing.'

'No. This is a ball. There has to be dancing.' And with a crooked smile, 'We're in a public place. We have an audience of thousands. I'm not going to break any rules *here.*'

This was reassuring. 'Okay, but if we dance, so do others,' she said as she spotted Jasmine and Kai peel away from a large group of people and head towards an unoccupied seating area. 'Kai needs to dance with Jasmine.'

'Why?'

'I'll explain later.' They'd reached the younger couple. Hallie smiled brightly. 'Anyone for dancing over by the balcony? I'm thinking it's probably the coolest place in the ballroom.'

Jasmine shrugged, glancing at Kai through lowered lashes. C'mon, Jasmine, Hallie willed the younger girl, this is the age of equality, *ask him.* But Jasmine stayed silent. And so did Kai.

'Smell me,' she said to Nick. 'How do I smell?'

Nick sighed, bent his head to her neck and sniffed. 'You smell divine.'

'Now you smell Jasmine,' she ordered Kai. 'Everything okay there?'

Jasmine lifted her chin. Kai nodded, a small smile playing around his lips.

'Excellent. And do I look beautiful?' she asked Nick.

'Extremely,' he said dryly.

'What about Jasmine?'

'She looks exquisite,' Nick assured her gravely, his eyes alight with laughter.

'So there's no problem in that direction either. Of course, I'm assuming that everyone here can dance. You *can* dance, can't you?' she asked Kai pointedly.

Kai knew when to give in gracefully. He gave Nick a man-to-man stare that was strangely sympathetic and then turned to bow gracefully to Jasmine before offering his arm. She took it, and together they moved off towards the dance floor.

'Your brothers have a lot to answer for,' said Nick with a rueful shake of his head. 'They've taught you man-handling skills a woman your age really shouldn't have. I shudder to think what you'll be like when you're older.'

'More subtle, I hope,' said Hallie, following Jasmine and Kai's progress though the throng of people with a frown. 'Look at them! He's not even touching her. Anyone would think he doesn't *want* to dance with her!'

'That would be my call,' said Nick. He was guiding her towards the dance floor as they spoke.

'Not that I have anything against you being right in general, but in this particular case I really hope you're wrong.' Matchmaking really wasn't her forte. What if Kai *wasn't* in love with the younger girl? What if she'd given Jasmine the wrong idea altogether? 'I can't watch.' She turned abruptly and came nose to chest with Nick's shirt. 'Out of my way. I'm going to go and shoot myself for interfering.'

'Wait,' said Nick, his hands on her shoulders as he urged her back around.

The other couple had started dancing and if Kai had thought to keep Jasmine at arm's length, Jasmine had other ideas. Her small hands slid up his arms to rest on his shoulders. Kai's hands rather unwillingly slid to her waist, his fingertips brushing the bare skin of her back and then, as if he couldn't help himself, he gathered her close, the tension and the longing in him unmistakable.

'My parents used to dance like that,' said Nick. 'They always gave each other room to move, to be themselves, but then when they came together you could tell that at that moment in time there was nowhere else they'd rather be. It was like…magic.'

'Nick, you're a romantic!' Hallie turned towards him, thoroughly enchanted by his words. 'Do you think *we're* going to dance like that?'

'No.' His voice was firm but his eyes were warm as he swung her smoothly into her arms. 'We are going to avoid dancing like that at all costs.'

He danced like a dream. As if he'd held her in his arms a hundred times before yet still delighted in the feel of her. The brush of a thigh, fingertips on bare skin; it was like foreplay, like flirting, and Nick was a master of both. It was his fault Hallie snuggled closer when a slow number began. His fault that she slowed it way down and let her body remember the feel of flesh on flesh and the pleasure his hands and lips could bring. He had the most wonderful touch, she thought dreamily, a lover's touch, and she savoured the moment and the man who gave it to her.

It could have been fifteen minutes later, it could have been fifty, when the music stopped and Nick peeled her out of his arms.

'I was having a Cinderella moment,' said Hallie, warmth creeping into her cheeks as she eyed Nick warily. 'It's possible I got a bit carried away.'

'It's all right,' said Nick with a heavy sigh. 'I'm getting used to it. Do you want to go out to the balcony?'

Where there was bound to be a night-time Hong Kong skyline to be dazzled by, rather than the man beside her. Hallie was all for it. 'Can you see Jasmine and Kai anywhere?'

'They left the dance floor half an hour ago.'

Hopefully this was a good thing.

There were almost as many people on the balcony as there were inside. The air was cooler, the faint breeze a welcome surprise. 'What time is it?' she asked him.

'Eleven-thirty. Not long to go now.'

No, it wasn't. Not to midnight. Not to the end of their time together. Hallie smiled, but it wasn't a real smile. It was going to hurt to say goodbye to this man in two days' time, she'd always thought it might. She just hadn't realized how much.

And then the thunder of drums sounded from inside and people turned and started heading inside, Jasmine amongst them. 'Lion dancing,' said the younger girl, linking arms with Hallie as they fell into step with the slow moving crowd.

'How was *your* dancing?' she asked and laughed when Jasmine blushed. 'Where's Kai?'

'Recovering,' said Jasmine impishly. 'Actually he's gone to the kitchen. Something to do with checking out the wait staff.'

The drums settled into a steady, driving rhythm and a magnificent Chinese lion appeared, bigger and more elaborate than Hallie had ever seen. He strutted, roared, and considered the poles set out before him, each pair of poles that little bit higher than the next. He disdained the lowest poles, sniffed at the next, wove his way through the third, and sat before the fourth. He groomed himself lazily, as he studied the tallest of the poles, poles that were taller than Nick, and then with a flick of his tail and an unbelievable leap he was standing on top of them and along with it all came the bold beating of drums. The colour red was everywhere; on decorations, on dresses, on the jackets of the wait staff who circulated with a never-ending supply of drinks and finger food. The wait staff. Hallie stared hard at a waiter heading towards them with an empty tray. He looked familiar, irritatingly familiar.

'Nick,' she whispered, disengaging her arm from Jasmine's and tugging on his sleeve. Wasn't that the waiter from the restaurant? The one who'd served the poisoned crab? 'Nick!' But Nick was engrossed in the lion dancing. And then the waiter was almost upon them, one hand holding the tray aloft, his other hand close to his side and in it was something that gleamed with a dull black shine. Nick was turning towards her now, but it was too late to warn him. If it was a gun, the waiter had a clear shot. Hallie did the only thing that came to mind.

She charged the approaching waiter and tackled him, gridiron style, and they went tumbling to the ground, both of them, the crowd parting as onlookers scrambled to get out of the way. Some were quick enough, others weren't. Two other guests hit the ground, both of them men, both of them cursing, but not nearly as much as Nick who was wading through the wreckage, trying to get to her. The waiter scrambled to his feet and rabbited his way through the crowd, his tray and whatever had been in his hand lying forgotten on the floor.

'It was the waiter from the crab restaurant! He was aiming something at you,' she said breathlessly as Nick helped her to her feet. Kai was beside them now, barking orders into a cell phone. 'I thought he had a gun!'

'You mean this?' said Kai, picking up a small black cylinder that gleamed dully.

It was metal. It was black. It looked like the barrel of a gun. But it wasn't a gun. She glanced at Nick to see how he was taking this latest development. Not well. 'It certainly *looked* like a gun,' she said with a cheesy smile. 'From a distance.'

'Actually, it is a gun of sorts,' said Kai. 'It dispenses darts.'

'Ah,' she said. 'Good to know.'

'Are you hurt?' asked Nick grimly.

Her head was pounding, her arm aching. It was five minutes to twelve. 'Hurt? Me? Of course not.'

Kai was making sure no one else was injured. Jasmine was soothing ruffled tempers. Nick was looking at her, his face set. 'I can't believe you crash-tackled him,' he said at last. 'Don't you have any concern for your own safety whatsoever? What were you *thinking?*'

'I was thinking of you!' she said heatedly. 'I thought he was going to shoot you! I couldn't just stand by and do *nothing.*'

'Um, excuse me,' said Jasmine tentatively, 'but I thought we might go and find my father and then get you both home. He's probably out on the balcony waiting for the fireworks to start.'

'Who needs to go outside?' muttered Hallie. 'They've already started in here.' But she followed Jasmine and Kai out to the balcony with Nick at her side and stood where Kai decided it was best to put them, backs to the wall in an alcove.

'*Another* attempt?' said John when he joined them and Kai told him of the waiter and the dart gun. 'I had hoped we were being overly suspicious.'

'I wish I knew who was behind it all,' said Nick.

'Yeah,' said Hallie glumly. 'Pity the waiter got away.' Lara Croft wouldn't have let the waiter get away. Lara Croft would have nailed the waiter and then they'd have *known* who was behind the attempts on Nick's life. 'I wasn't really thinking straight when I tackled that waiter,' she told Nick apologetically.

'Finally, she sees reason,' he murmured.

'I should have pinned him down.'

Nick stared at her incredulously. John Tey smothered a chuckle.

'I have our people looking for him,' said Kai. 'We'll find him.'

People were crowding onto the balcony. It was almost midnight, and, as far as the Chinese were concerned, the start of a bright new year. As far as Hallie was concerned it was the end of a long day with more ups and downs in it than a triple-loop roller coaster. 'Two more minutes,' she said, glancing at the glowing neon clock set high on the hotel wall.

'I shall wish for a better new year for you,' Jasmine told Nick earnestly. 'One without assassins.'

'Thanks, Jasmine.' Nick's features softened before hardening again as his gaze rested challengingly on Hallie. 'You could try wishing for some more sense.'

Ha! Hallie smiled sweetly. 'My wish is that the vase I bought you turns up tomorrow.' Then she could stuff him in it.

'What vase?' said Kai, his head snapping round as he pinned her with his gaze.

'The one I bought for him at Lucky Plaza,' she said. 'When you and Jasmine were in the bathroom.' Kai was looking at her in disbelief. 'Separate bathrooms,' she added hastily. 'As opposed to being together in the same bathroom.'

'You bought a vase,' said Kai. 'For Nick. From the corner shop near the bathrooms in Lucky Plaza.'

Hallie nodded.

'A funeral vase.'

Hallie nodded again. 'Yes, that's right. The one in the window.'

'And the salesman *let* you?' said Kai.

'Well, he took some persuading, but, yes. I arranged to have it delivered before the New Year, but it hasn't arrived.'

Kai was turning to John, shaking his head and muttering something. John was staring at her, open-mouthed, as if frozen to the spot. Nick and Jasmine looked as baffled by their reactions as Hallie felt.

'What?' she said uneasily. 'What's wrong?'

Ten. The countdown to midnight began in Cantonese.

Nine. 'The shop you speak of sells funeral vases, sure enough,' said John.

Eight. 'But they don't sell them empty.'

Seven. 'What do you mean, not empty?' she said.

Six. 'The one I bought was empty.'

Five. 'Well, they don't deliver them empty,' said Kai.

Four. 'When you bought Nick that vase…

Three. '…you ordered his execution.'

Two. 'I *what*?'

One. 'That's why someone's been trying to kill him.'

Oh, dear.

The crowd roared as fireworks erupted in the sky, huge blasts of colour raining down from the heavens, each one more spectacular than the last, and all around them people were laughing and embracing, kissing and shaking hands, their faces alight with pleasure and the glow from the fireworks.

She opened her mouth to speak but no words came out. They were all staring at her: Jasmine, Kai, Nick and John; all waiting for her to speak, but she had no idea what to say. Her hands were trembling, hell, her entire body was trembling with a mixture of fear and disbelief. This was a joke, right? It had to be a joke. But the expression on Kai's face assured her it wasn't.

A fresh blast of fireworks opened up the sky with a crack that made her jump; a kaleidoscope of red, green and gold, while her gut roiled and her head ached with the sure knowledge that in buying Nick that damned vase, she'd made a huge and deadly mistake.

'I—' What on earth *could* she say? She looked to Nick. 'You—' Nope, she still couldn't find any words. She put a hand to her aching head and shrugged, still helplessly enmeshed in Nick's gaze. Good Lord, she'd put a contract out on him. How the hell was she supposed to explain *that*?

She couldn't. Not now. Maybe not ever. It was just too bizarre.

But they were all still waiting. Waiting for her to say something. Anything. She opened her mouth and took a deep breath. 'Sorry about that,' she said finally.

CHAPTER EIGHT

HALLIE had never pegged Nick as the coldly furious type and he wasn't. His was more of a simmering, bubbling fury and only his iron control, and quite possibly the presence of Kai and the Teys, kept it contained. They'd left as soon as the fireworks were over and the drive home had been mercifully conversation-free. Once at the villa she and Nick had said their thank yous and their goodnights and headed for the bedroom, and once they were *there*, Nick wasted no time in shrugging off his jacket and tie and opening a couple of shirt buttons.

Hallie eyed him warily as she set her purse down on the counter and folded her wrap. Her brothers had tempers, all of them. She was no stranger to eruptions of the masculine variety. Pete's was like a summer storm, all noise and flash and gone in an instant. Luke's involved pacing, pointing and a great deal of arm-waving. Jake's was controlled and biting, and Tris... Tris didn't do temper very often, but when he did he flayed people raw. Hallie was hoping, really hoping, that Nick was going to be a little less like Tris and a lot more like any one of her other brothers in that regard.

A timid knock sounded on the door and Hallie opened it to find Jasmine standing there holding a tea tray.

'Peppermint tea,' said the younger girl, pressing the tray into her hands. 'It's very soothing,' she added, and fled.

'I knew it,' said Nick as Hallie nudged the door closed and set the tea tray on the sideboard. He was pacing now, from one end of the room to the other. This was good. Pacing she could deal with. Pacing expended energy that could otherwise be used for yelling. Tris never paced.

'I should *never* have gone shoe-shopping with my mother,' he was saying now. 'She's a bad influence. I should have gone to the country club and found Bridget instead. Bridget would have pretended to be my wife for a week. She'd have ripped Jasmine to shreds, alienated John, tried to seduce Kai, and driven me insane, but so what? At least she wouldn't have *ordered my execution*!'

Uh, oh. He'd stopped pacing. 'Tea?' she offered.

'Why me?' he roared. 'Why you? Why *now*? Do you know how close we are to securing this deal? Do you have *any* idea how much it's worth?'

She knew. 'I have a plan,' she said quickly.

'No! No more plans. I know your plans and they *never, ever work*!

'Are you sure you wouldn't like some tea?' Hallie sniffed a steaming cup. 'I think she put alcohol in it.'

He stared at her. Stared at the tea.

'I'm calling your brothers,' he said abruptly. 'I'm going to tell them all about this man, wife and funeral-vase fiasco and then I'm going to get them to come and take you home.'

'You can't,' she said pleadingly. 'You need me.'

'To do *what*?' He was back to roaring.

'To go back to the shop and cancel the hit.'

He stared at her in disbelief. And then, 'No! Absolutely not! These people are professional killers, Hallie. They're not going to be impressed by you saying you made a mistake and didn't realize you were ordering my execution after all. They'll kill you to keep you quiet.'

'I'm not going to tell them I made a mistake,' said Hallie. 'I'm going to tell them I needed the job done before New Year and that they failed to deliver. I'm going to tell them that the terms of our contract have been breached and that I no longer need their services.'

'You're going to *fire* them?'

'Yes.'

'I don't believe this, ' he muttered. 'It's like living in a black comedy. I'm calling your brother. The dangerous one. Maybe he'll know how to handle you. What's his number?'

'I can't tell you,' said Hallie. 'Well, I could, but then I'd have to kill you.'

'Get in line,' he snapped. 'What's the number?'

'You can't have it.'

'Then I'll ring every dojo in Singapore until I find your other brother. Or every charter plane operation in Greece. Yes, that might be best. That brother can probably get *here faster*!'

'No! Listen to me, Nick. I can fix this. First thing in the morning.'

'It's New Year's Day, remember? The shop won't even be open.'

'Maybe not the shop,' she agreed. 'But they'll be contactable somehow. Kai will know how it's done. We'll ask him.'

'This would be the Kai who took you to the plaza and let you buy the vase in the first place.'

'To be fair, he didn't know I'd bought it,' said Hallie. 'He's Jasmine's bodyguard, not mine. But I'm sure he'd agree to help.'

Nick was pacing again. Muttering beneath his breath and raking his hand through his hair. Very Luke. She opened her mouth to explain her idea some more.

'No.' He held up his hand for silence. 'Don't talk. Don't say another word. Let me think.'

So she closed her mouth and concentrated on pouring the tea and stirring in sugar, lots of sugar, to help with the shock. She was shakier than she wanted to admit, horrified by the notion that she'd inadvertently ordered Nick's execution. She'd wanted to make her own mistakes, sure enough, but she'd wanted to make her own *little* mistakes. Not huge, deadly ones she wasn't at all sure she was going to be able to fix. 'I'll call Tris if that's what you want,' she offered quietly. 'I can call him now.'

Nick shot her a hard-eyed glare and Hallie looked away, looked at her tea. She was going to cry, dammit, she could feel the tears building behind her eyes. She put her hand to her cheek and hastily wiped away the first escapee. Another followed.

'No crying!' said Nick hurriedly. 'I don't do crying.'

'I'm so sorry, Nick. I've ruined everything for you.'

'Not yet, you haven't. Let's think about this. Maybe it *is* as simple as cancelling the contract. We could call them. Get them to meet us at the shop. Let them know we're coming in and that plans have changed.'

'We? What we? There is no *we* because *you* can't come!' She wouldn't let him come. 'If I walk you into that shop they'll shoot you on the spot and *stuff* you into that vase before I can say good morning. I need to go there alone.'

'No.' One word, simple and irrevocable.

'You can't come. You have to pretend you don't know anything about it. If they think I'm cancelling their services because they botched the job and you discovered I ordered your execution, they may well kill you anyway. Out of sheer professional pride.'

'How much alcohol did you say was in that tea?' he asked.

Hallie passed him a cup and he swallowed the contents in one go.

'I hate this,' he muttered.

'Yes, but it'll work,' she said with far more confidence than she felt. 'Trust me.'

'I do trust you,' he said. 'It's the bad guys I don't trust. What if your luck runs out? What if you get hurt? I'd never forgive myself.'

'You have to think positive,' she said. 'Think Lara Croft in Tomb Raider.'

'Lara Croft has big guns and multiple lives. You have no guns and one life.'

'To live the way I choose. I choose to do this, Nick. This is my mistake. I want to fix it.'

He was closer now, close enough to reach out and touch, and the conflict between wanting to keep her safe and wanting to agree with her plan was there in his eyes. He lifted his hand to her cheek, his eyes almost black, his tension a living thing.

'I can't do this,' he muttered roughly.

'Which *this* are we talking about?' she whispered as his lips came closer to her own and his hand slid from her cheek to cup the back of her head. 'This as in kissing or this as in agreeing to my plan?'

'Any of this,' he said, and captured her lips with his own.

She expected anger from him, the remains of it at any rate, but his kiss was unexpectedly sweet, his hands in her hair so very gentle as he traced the bump on her head.

'Does it still hurt?' he murmured roughly.

'No.' She slid her hands over his chest, luxuriating in the feel of him, so warm and solid and, above all, alive. He kissed her again, deeper this time with a needy edge to it that she matched with a helpless, aching need of her own.

'How about now?'

'No.' With her hands digging into his shoulders and her skin on fire from his touch. She had no defences from this man, not one, but still she tried to dissuade him, for his sake as well as her own. 'You're breaking all the rules,' she whispered as his hands slid to her shoulders and his long, sure fingers started toying with the straps of her gown. 'A bedroom is definitely not a public place.'

'I know.' In that gravelly bedroom voice that set a woman to shuddering all by itself.

'And the door is shut and the curtains are drawn.'

'No audience,' he muttered, and set his lips to her shoulder in the exact place her straps had been.

'And I don't know about you,' she said desperately, in a last-ditch effort to remind him of the rules, 'but this is really starting to feel like sex to me.'

'It's not sex,' he said with utter certainty. 'It's fore-play.'

Hallie gave in, gave up, shivering in pleasure as his mouth feathered over her shoulder, tracing a slow, tor-turous path along her collar-bone. He lifted her effort-lessly onto the counter and found her nipple with his mouth, through the thin barrier of silk that her dress afforded her, but it wasn't enough, not nearly enough. She wove her fingers through his hair, revelling in its soft, silky texture as she arched back and he slid the straps of her dress down her arms. The bodice fol-lowed and then her breasts were bared for him and his fingers grazed her puckered nipples with a touch so gentle she didn't know whether to weep with pleasure or scream with frustration. 'I won't break,' she said huskily, by way of a hint.

'I know that too.' His smile was crooked. 'You're probably indestructible. I noticed that today. It's just that you look so damn fragile.'

'I'm not fragile,' she said. 'I'm not even a virgin any more.' And then he bit down on her aching, swollen breasts and she screamed her approval as sensation shot through her.

'God help us,' he said fervently as he swept her into his arms and carried her over to the bed.

Hallie clung to him as they tumbled onto the pillows, wanting him over her, inside of her, wanting it now. Her heart beat wildly and her breathing was fast and urgent as she undid the buttons on his shirt, pushed it aside, and surged against him, glorying in the rasp of skin on skin as her nipples pressed hard and tight against his muscled chest. More, she craved it, demanded it, fumbling with his belt, with the fastening of his trousers, only to have him push her hand aside with a half-strangled laugh.

'No,' he muttered. 'Ladies first.'

'Whatever happened to equality?' she grumbled.

'Equality is overrated.' His smile was slow and wicked as he eased her gown from her body and then her panties. 'Ladies first is a good option for you right now. Trust me.' He took her hands and drew them above her head and she let him do it, let him do whatever he wanted. She was naked for him, utterly naked except for the diamonds at her ears and around her throat. She felt completely exposed, utterly vulnerable as he loomed over her, his eyes intent. 'Close your eyes,' he whispered and she did as he commanded, whimpering with pleasure as his lips traced a path from her wrist to her elbow. He stopped when he reached her elbow, stopped to curse beneath his breath before tracing the area surrounding the angry red graze with gentle fingers. Hallie shivered hard and he moved on, his hands tracing a path down her body for his lips to follow, the soft underside of her breast, the slight curve of her stomach, and everywhere he touched her muscles contracted and the pleasure built. She knew what was coming when he spread her thighs wide and moved lower, knew it and craved it but he made her wait, made her plead while he scattered tiny kisses over her hips and his thumb circled the sensitive folds of her flesh.

'Please!' As his mouth moved closer and his hands held her firm. She strained against him, clutched at the sheet above her head, and finally, finally, he licked into her. She couldn't breathe, the heat of his mouth was divine, the rhythmic stroking of his tongue an unbearably exquisite torment. He knew exactly where to lick, exactly how to please her, and she writhed beneath him, riding the wave of anticipation he built so cleverly, riding it hard. And when she didn't think she could stand any more, when she was slick with sweat and just about to shatter into a million pieces, he concentrated his efforts and the world exploded inside her, all around her, as she shuddered her release.

'Oh, my God!' she gasped.

'Told you so,' he muttered, shedding his trousers and moving over her as she brought her hands to his hair and his lips down to hers for a feverish kiss that had nothing to do with tenderness and everything to do with raw, driving need. It was his turn to groan now, his turn to shudder as he settled himself between her legs. His turn to whimper as her need for him turned savage.

'Shh,' he muttered. 'Easy.'

Nick inched slowly into her, inexorably penetrating her hot, slippery flesh as her body stretched to accommodate him. He slid his fingers between them to further coax her taut, tight muscles into submission. And then he was seated in her up to the hilt, exactly where he wanted to be, his entire body on the verge of exploding as her hips slammed into his and her body climaxed around him again. He'd never seen anything more wanton, more beautiful, than Hallie lost in passion. So fearless, so utterly open for him as he spread her legs wide, cupped his hands around her buttocks and surged into her, glorying in his possession, in the scent of sex, and the tight slickness encasing him.

'This would be the sex part,' she whispered as her legs encircled his waist and her nails raked his back.

'This isn't sex.' He was spiralling out of control, seconds away from his own pulsing release. 'This is madness.'

Hallie woke just before dawn, too worried about what the day held to go back to sleep. She slid out of bed and padded to the window to look down on the Teys' tranquil garden, wondering if John would be up soon and out there practising t'ai chi. Wondering if he did and if she watched, would some of his calm feed through to her? She shifted the curtains aside to lay her palm on the window-pane, and reached for the confidence she knew she had to have if her plan was ever going to work.

Nick stirred and she turned to watch him; saw him reach for her, and wake when he couldn't find her. She felt the moment he saw her, felt it as a heat that licked over her entire body, and then he was out of bed and heading towards her, beautifully, magnificently naked. She knew that body now, had loved every inch of it during the night. She knew his scent, the taste of him on her tongue, the playful edge in him and the fire.

What she didn't know was the workings of his mind. What he wanted from her and whether he was going to regret their lovemaking and pull back as he had done last time and, in doing so, shatter her heart. So she looked to his eyes to see if they were cool, to his mouth to see if it was stern, and to his jaw to see if it was set, but Nick was none of those things this morning. He snaked an arm around her waist and drew her into his warmth and his hardness, resting his chin on her head, saying nothing as he too stared out at the wakening day.

'I couldn't sleep,' she murmured.

'I noticed,' he rumbled, his voice working its usual magic on her skin. 'Ready to save the day?'

Not yet. But she would be. 'Sure.'

'Liar,' he countered, with a gruffness that spoke of worry. 'You don't have to do this, you know. It's not too late to change your mind. We can find another way. A safer way.'

'There is no safe way. This is a good plan, Nick. You know it is. I want to give it a try. I want to fix this my way.'

'Why? So you can prove to your brothers that you can?'

'No. It's not that.' All her life her brothers had fixed her mistakes when she'd made them. They'd done it out of love for her; she knew that. They'd done it because they considered her upbringing their job and they took their work seriously. But hadn't they seen? Hadn't they ever looked beneath the protests and seen how they were eroding her confidence and her self-belief? 'This isn't about my brothers,' she said quietly. 'It's about me. I need to prove to myself that I can do this.'

Nick sighed heavily, his arms tightening around her. 'Can't we just take that as a given?'

'No.'

'Damn.' He turned her in his arms, turned so that she was facing him, then lifted his hand to tuck a stray strand of hair behind her ear. 'How can I help?' he murmured. 'What do you need?'

No more questions, no more protest, just simple support and it flew like a shaft, straight and true, to lodge itself in her heart. She'd been walking a tight-rope ever since she'd met this man. She'd resisted his warmth and resisted his wit. She'd even resisted his lovemaking for a while. But she couldn't resist his belief in her. There would be no more balancing on the high wire, not with this man. Silently, willingly, Hallie tumbled into love. 'What do I need?' Her lips curved as she wound her hands in his hair and pulled his lips down to meet her own. The answer was obvious.

Right now, right this very minute, she needed him.

CHAPTER NINE

'I HATE this,' said Nick five hours later as everyone gathered in the Teys' kitchen for a final briefing of the plan. 'I can't believe I'm letting you do this.'

'It's the only way,' said John Tey. 'She's the only one who can cancel the contract. I'm afraid your accompanying her is out of the question.'

Nick scowled. The thought of Hallie facing down professional assassins without him ate away at his stomach like acid.

'I still think I should be going there on my own,' said Hallie. 'Completely on my own.'

'No,' he said curtly. 'You are *not* going there alone. If not me, then Kai.'

'Why drag Kai into it? Or John, for that matter? This business has nothing to do with them.'

'No,' he repeated. 'You take Kai or you don't go at all.'

'Kai will accompany you,' said John.

'He's very capable,' said Jasmine earnestly.

Hallie sighed and glared at him, glared at them all. 'Fine, I'll take Kai.'

Nick met Kai's steady gaze and a look of silent understanding passed between them. Kai would do everything in his power to protect her. Everything. He'd better.

'Stop that,' Hallie told him sharply.

'Stop what?'

'That look. The one that says you're going to tear strips off Kai's hide if he lets anything happen to me.'

'You *know* that look?'

'I have four brothers,' she reminded him darkly.

'And I can honestly say I don't know how any of them survived your adolescence,' he snapped.

John Tey smiled. Kai's cough sounded suspiciously like laughter. 'I've phoned ahead. The meeting is set,' said John. 'They'll be waiting for you at the shop.'

'Ready?' Nick asked her quietly.

'Ready,' she said with far more confidence than the situation warranted. 'My negotiating skills are honed and ready to go.'

They ought to be. He, Kai, John and Jasmine had spent the last two hours firing every conceivable question or objection the bad guys might come up with at her and coaching her on her reply. 'Stick to the plan,' he said gruffly. 'Stay with Kai.'

'Of course.' Hallie smiled at him reassuringly.

'And don't do anything stupid.'

Her eyes narrowed. Her chin came up. He loved that look. 'Was there anything else?' she said, heavy on the sarcasm.

'Yeah.' He strode over to where she was standing,

took her face in his hands and kissed her with enough heat to light up half the city. 'Be careful.' He put his hands in his pockets and took a step back before he grabbed her again. Because if he did he knew he'd never let her go.

'It'll take twenty minutes to get there,' said Kai. 'Another twenty, perhaps, to complete the negotiation. I'll call when we're done.'

Nick nodded and watched in tight-lipped silence as they headed for the door. Watched while his stomach roiled for fear she'd be hurt, and his brain informed him that letting her attempt to cancel the hit out of some crazy desire to prove her worth was undoubtedly the worst decision he'd ever made.

It was going to be the longest forty minutes of his life.

It was New Year's Day and most of the shops were closed. Lucky Plaza was closed as well, but Kai drove directly to loading bay entrance number five, parked the Mercedes beside the huge, corrugated Roll-A-Door and cut the engine.

'They're meeting us here,' he said, nodding towards a wall-mounted security camera. 'They'll have seen us arrive. Are you ready?'

Hallie nodded. Her heart was beating a furious tattoo, her hands were clammy, and her lipstick had doubtless been chewed away completely, but she was ready. 'Wait!' Her lipstick. She flipped the sunshield of the car down to reveal the small mirror on the other side, fished her lipstick from her Hermès handbag and carefully applied a fresh coat to her lips. *Now* she was ready.

Kai gave her one of his rare, slow smiles and then the loading bay door opened and two suited sentries stood waiting for them. Hallie took a deep breath and then another before reaching for the door handle. She could do this. Would do this, dammit, because this little catastrophe was of *her* making and *she* was going to fix it. What was more, Nick *trusted* her to fix it.

It was time to go do business.

The plaza was deserted and eerily quiet, but the door to the little corner shop was open, the lights inside were on, and the young salesman she'd bought the vase from stood waiting by the counter. He wasn't alone. An older man with greying hair and hard black eyes stood beside him. Whoever he was, and she really wasn't inclined to ask, he wore authority like a cloak and power as if he was born to it. Maybe he was.

'Thank you for agreeing to see me at such short notice,' she said politely.

'We have no quarrel with the Tey organization,' the older man said in heavily clipped English. 'We prefer to keep it that way.' His cold black gaze shifted to Kai and then returned to her. 'You have business with us?'

'Business that should have been concluded by now,' said Hallie smoothly, knowing instinctively that this man would not tolerate weakness. 'I now find myself in the rather unfortunate position of having to change my plans.' She smiled, a careful, charming smile. 'I'm afraid your services are no longer required.'

'I'm afraid, Mrs Cooper, that we do not renegotiate contracts. Not even with those who place them,'

said the older man with a charming smile of his own.
'It's bad for business.'

Nick kept himself occupied by pacing from one end of
the Teys' long living room to the other. Jasmine had
made tea, two lots of tea, and thirty minutes had come
and gone. The first twenty had been bearable. The first
twenty minutes had involved Hallie and Kai getting to
where they were going. Now it was different. Now,
thought Nick grimly, Hallie was meeting with contract
killers, firing them, to be precise, and Nick's nerves
were stretched to breaking-point. Any time now,
they'd call.

'Your wife is a very resourceful woman,' said John.
John, who had been a quiet, reassuring presence
throughout the entire debacle. 'I'm confident she'll succeed. And Kai is with her. They will not dismiss him
lightly. Not the man, nor the organization he represents.'

Nick sighed heavily and ran a hand through his hair.
His primary concern was for Hallie's safety. Once she
was safe he would worry about the next problem,
namely that Kai's presence at the meeting and the
implied involvement of Tey Enterprises would have
unwanted consequences for the older man. 'How far
will this place you in their debt?'

'Not that far,' said John with a slight smile. 'We are
neither enemies nor allies, our two organizations, even
though both wield a great deal of power. We coexist.
We are respectful of each other. I do not believe this
small transaction will upset that balance.'

Nick didn't know whether to believe the other man

or not. His explanation sounded too simple and far too easy, given what he knew of Chinese culture. 'Let's hope you're right,' he said wearily. 'I know it's a risk, but I couldn't let her go alone.'

'Nor I,' said John. 'I am your host. I allowed my daughter to take your wife to Lucky Plaza in the first place. My conscience would not allow it.'

'Thank you,' said Nick quietly. He appreciated everything the older man had done for them. He really did.

'Your wife made a simple mistake,' said John magnanimously. 'It could have happened to anyone.'

Nick just stared at him.

'Okay,' said John. 'Maybe not anyone.'

'Of course you don't renegotiate contracts,' said Hallie, deciding it was time to examine a magnificent porcelain vase displayed on a marble pedestal. 'These really are the most exquisite pieces,' she said admiringly, and then, on a more businesslike note, 'I understand your position perfectly, but I'm not here to renegotiate. The delivery was not made in the specified time. Our contract is void. I have no need of another.' She was politeness itself. Tris would be proud of her. Nick would be amazed. 'I simply wished to let you know in person that I consider our business complete.'

He wasn't going to go for it. Hallie held the older man's gaze steadily, knowing in her bones that he was going to say that he didn't do this either. That the contract was complete when the delivery was made and not before. That was good business too.

'This is the first time we have had such a problem,' said the older man bleakly as he looked to the young salesman. 'Make it the last.'

The young crime lieutenant nodded respectfully.

The old general studied her thoughtfully before glancing once more at the silent Kai. 'So be it,' he said, with a dismissive wave of his hand. 'The contract is void. Happy New Year, Mrs Cooper. May it be a healthy and prosperous one for you and *all* your family. My assistant will see to the details.'

'Thank you,' said Hallie and bowed her head in acknowledgement because, frankly, it seemed the thing to do. She waited until the older man was gone before straightening and turning towards the salesman who'd sold her the vase in the first place.

'You're a very fortunate woman, Mrs Cooper,' he said dryly. 'He let you live.'

'Maybe he's turning over a New Year's leaf,' said Hallie.

Kai winced. The young salesman smiled his crooked smile. 'I like you,' he said.

'Be grateful you're not married to her,' said Kai.

'True.'

Hallie ignored their bonding banter completely. She wasn't done yet. 'Can you see to the details today?' she asked the salesman. 'Can you see to them now?' She watched as he whipped out his Palm pilot and pulled up his calendar.

'No problem,' he said. 'I will arrange to meet my contacts within the hour.'

Contacts, assassins, whatever. As long as he called

them off. 'Thank you,' she said, bestowing a brilliant smile on him, and then as a new thought occurred to her, 'I wonder...'

'No!' said Kai. 'No wondering.'

'No refunds either,' said the salesman.

'Of course not,' said Hallie. 'That would be tacky. I was just wondering about the vase. The vase in the window. After all, it *was* part of our arrangement...'

'They haven't called,' said Nick. 'What's taking them so long?' He was on his fourth cup of sugar-loaded green tea and the sugar was starting to take effect. Soon. They would call soon. Meanwhile Nick paced. Pacing was good. Pacing and waiting was far better than sitting and waiting and he wished for the hundredth time that he could have gone with her. Dammit, he *should* have gone with her, regardless. Because if anything happened to her...

The muffled ringing of John's cell phone interrupted his latest what if. Nick felt the blood drain from his face, felt an icy calm steal over him as John took the call. It was brusque, it was brief, it was in Cantonese. And then it was over.

John Tey pocketed his cell phone and turned towards him, a broad smile on his face. 'The meeting was a success. The contract has been dissolved.'

Nick felt the breath he'd been holding leave his body, felt the blood in his body start to move again as relief washed through him. Hallie was safe; that was all that mattered. His hands were trembling so he put them on the counter to make them stop; his legs were shaky too—nothing he could do about that other than pray they held him up until the sensation passed.

'Here,' said John, pressing a squat glass of clear liquid into his unresisting hand. 'You love her; you feared for her. It's a perfectly normal reaction.'

Nick drained the contents of the glass, almost choked on the fire of it. 'What *is* this stuff?' he spluttered between gasps.

'Cheap Russian vodka,' said John Tey with a chuckle. 'Very good for shock. Very good reminder that you are alive.'

'She did it,' said Jasmine joyfully. 'She's a hero.'

'Crazy, reckless woman,' Nick muttered beneath his breath. 'I should *never* have let her even attempt it.' Just wait until he got his hands on her. Wait till she walked through that door. Hero or not, he was going to lock her up and throw away the key until she *swore* she'd never put him through anything like that again!

'Of course, you're a hero too,' said Jasmine thoughtfully. 'You may actually be the biggest hero here today.'

'What?' Nick blinked. How could *he* be a hero? He'd done *nothing!* Nothing but wait and in waiting go slowly insane.

'You didn't interfere,' said Jasmine. 'You let her go even though it went against your nature to do so and you trusted her to fix the problem herself. I think that was very heroic.'

'You're a sweetheart,' he said gently as he held out his empty glass for another hit. 'But I think you're confusing heroism with lunacy.'

* * *

Twenty minutes later Hallie and Kai walked through the door and Nick managed to greet them civilly enough, thanks in no small part to John's most excellent cheap Russian vodka.

'All done,' said Hallie, all smiles. 'I told you it would work.'

Nick sighed, reached for her and held her close to his heart and she sagged against him, not quite as nonchalant or as confident as she seemed.

'Don't you ever put me through that again,' he said gruffly. 'You hear me?'

Hallie hugged him hard and pulled back a little self-consciously.

Jasmine, he noted, was playing it far cooler with Kai. She'd waited until he set the large parcel he was carrying down on the sideboard before crossing to greet him, a fragrant cup of tea held carefully in both hands. He watched as Kai took the tea with a wry smile on his face and a gentle meeting of hands and knew Hallie had been right about that too. It was a pretty sight, two dark heads bent over an offering of tea, with whitewashed walls, dark wooden furniture and a hastily wrapped parcel in the background. A hastily wrapped *vase*-shaped parcel in the background.

No. No way. She wouldn't have dared. Temper licked through him, hot and swift. It couldn't possibly be what he thought it was. Could it? He glared at Hallie and she smiled back at him, the picture of innocence. He didn't trust that smile, not one little bit. 'What the *hell*,' he said, pointing towards the parcel, 'is *that*?'

* * *

Nick accepted John's rather hasty offer to complete their business directly. It was either that or blow a fuse over how and why Hallie came to be in possession of that damned vase, and he suspected the older man knew it. So they were in John's study, the contract papers spread out on the desk, having just been signed by the older man and just about to be signed by him. Trouble was, he couldn't do it.

'Is there a problem?' asked the older man.

'Yes,' he said.

'We have agreed that the terms are fair.' John's voice was cool.

'And they are,' Nick was quick to say. 'That's not the problem. The problem is that a contract is based on trust and understanding. Honour. You've always been honourable in your dealings with me. I, on the other hand, have not been completely honourable in my dealings with you.'

John Tey sat back in his chair and regarded him steadily.

Nick took a deep breath and prepared to tell it as it was. 'I'm not married. Hallie isn't my wife. She's only pretending to be my wife.'

'I know,' said the older man, and at Nick's open-mouthed astonishment, 'I've always known.'

Maybe it was the vodka, maybe it was this latest shock coming so close on the heels of the appearance of the vase, but Nick didn't know what to say. Or do. He wasn't entirely sure he still had the power of speech.

'You don't really think I'd sign a multimillion-dollar deal with a man and not run a background check on him, do you? It's standard company procedure.' John Tey smiled. 'Given that the company details you provided were accurate to the last cent, I would, however, like to know why you felt it necessary to lie about your marital status.'

Ah. 'A misjudgement on my part,' said Nick uncomfortably. He really didn't want to go into the why of it.

'I believe that at one stage my daughter viewed you as a prospective husband,' said the older man shrewdly. 'And that you invented a wife because you wished to spare her feelings.'

'I invented a wife because I wanted to secure this deal,' corrected Nick, with a self-mocking twist of his lips. If he was going to tell the truth it may as well be the unvarnished truth. 'I didn't want to marry your daughter and I couldn't afford to offend either of you. Trust me, there was far more self-preservation involved than chivalry.'

John conceded the point with a shrug. 'Then there's Hallie.' He shook his head, smothered a chuckle. 'You may not be married to her yet, Nicholas, but it's clear you've given her your heart.'

'What?' spluttered Nick. 'You can't think... I'm not...' Oh, hell! He was.

He was foolishly, undeniably in love with Hallie Bennett. She of the Titian hair, golden brown eyes, and God-given *talent* for finding trouble.

'I think you're going to have your hands full there, son.'

Nick groaned. He could see it all so clearly. Hallie in his bed, sharing his life, and him never wanting, never even *looking* at another woman because this one filled him so completely. He could see it now. A house brimful with ancient wonders and rambunctious sons, and a tiny daughter with fly-away black hair and golden eyes and the ability to wrap her daddy, uncles and all of her brothers around her dainty little fingers. He'd be buying shotguns by the dozen. Valium by the caseful. What if—and here was a truly terrifying thought—what if they had *two* daughters? 'Shoot me now,' he told John. 'It'll be quicker and far less painful.'

'Oh, I don't think so,' countered John. 'I think you'll find yourself well satisfied with your choice of life partner. Besides, I can hardly do business with a dead man, now can I?' John picked up the pen and passed it to him. 'My signature is already on the papers, Nicholas. Honour has been satisfied. Sign.'

Hallie left Nick and John downstairs finalizing the distribution deal and headed to the suite to start packing for the trip home. The packing could have waited until later in the day, tomorrow even, but she was too wired to rest so she started on it with a vengeance. The plan had worked beautifully, Nick was safe, and there was a quiet satisfaction in knowing that no one had pushed her aside and stepped in to save the day. She could be proud of that. Would be proud of it, dammit, and not apologetic as Nick seemed to think she should be, although, to be fair, it wasn't the successful cancellation of the hit that had sent Nick into orbit; it was the presence of the vase. Nick wasn't real happy about the vase.

Truth be told, Nick wasn't real happy with *her*.

She'd been a lousy corporate wife, distracting him from his work, arranging to have him killed, and bringing his contract negotiations to a standstill. He was probably counting the hours until they touched down in London so he could pay her and be rid of her. Not that she blamed him.

For her part, saying goodbye to Nick and watching him walk away was going to be the hardest thing she'd ever done. One step forward, two steps back. For all her newfound self-confidence she knew instinctively that letting Nick go was going to break her heart.

But she was determined that there would be no tears, no telling him she loved him. No. She wouldn't do that to him. He'd wanted a wife for a week and after that week was over he wanted that wife to leave. That was the deal they'd agreed on; she could at least get that right.

She was still packing ten minutes later when Nick came up to the room and was composed enough to greet him with a tentative smile, a smile that faded when it wasn't returned. She watched him cross to the window and stand there, grim and preoccupied, with his hands in his pocket and his back towards her. Oh, hell. Something was wrong. She waited for him to say something, *anything*, but he remained ominously silent.

Hallie picked up a shirt and attempted to fold it, but her fingers wouldn't co-operate. She had to know. 'Did he sign?'

'Yeah, he signed.'

Thank goodness for that! Hallie let out the breath she'd been holding. For a moment there she'd thought she'd sabotaged his business deal completely. But if that wasn't it, then why the silent treatment?

Oh, yeah. The vase. 'I, ah, packed the vase for you. I thought I'd carry it in my hand luggage. It's very fragile.'

He closed his eyes, muttered a curse.

'And very good value as well,' she said in a rush. 'I think when you have it valued you'll be pleasantly surprised. It's functional too.'

At this, his eyes opened and fixed on her, thoroughly disbelieving.

'Not that I expect you to, ah, use it in that way. You could use it as a regular vase. You could put flowers in it.'

'Flowers,' he repeated.

'Maybe a dried arrangement of some kind,' she suggested.

'I'll keep that in mind.'

She nodded. 'Yes, well, I'm really glad the whole funeral-vase shambles didn't ruin it for you. I think, given the circumstances, that it might be better if I don't take your money. I mean, what with the clothes you provided and the trip itself...'

The contract hit...

'What do you mean *not take the money*? You have to take the money.' Nick pinned her with an angry gaze. 'We had an agreement.'

So they did. Hallie bit her lip and looked away.

'You need that money to finish your diploma.'

The diploma. Hallie sighed. Right now the diploma

didn't seem to be very important at all. Maybe it wasn't. 'I'm thinking of putting my studies on hold.'

'Why?'

'I've had an idea.'

'God help us all,' he muttered. And then, as if bracing himself for a hurricane, 'Continue.'

'I'm going to start my own business.'

'What kind of business?'

'I want to start dealing in Asian antiquities, ceramics to be more specific. I have the knowledge. I know what I'm looking for. Not quite tomb raiding, I know, but I think I'd be good at it.' She waited for a great guffaw of mocking laughter, but it didn't come.

'Will you have enough start-up money?' he asked. 'Will ten thousand pounds be enough?'

'I'm going to start small. Approach a few collectors and find out what they're buying. Then see if I can find it for them.'

'Because if you need more, I'd be more than willing to back your business venture.'

'You'd do that? Even after all the trouble I've caused you?'

'Yes. You have what it takes to succeed no matter what you do. I've told you that before.'

Hallie's eyes filled with tears. He was making it hard, so hard, for her to let him go. Not like her brothers at all, this man before her. Freedom, equality, respect; he'd shown her them all. If only he'd fallen in love with her as well…

But he hadn't. And if they became business partners she'd never be able to keep her feelings for him a secret and *then* where would they be? 'Thank you,' she said huskily. 'Your support means a lot to me but I need to do this on my own.'

Nick nodded. 'I can understand that. But if you ever need help you'll call me.'

'Sure.' Never. She closed the lid on her bulging suitcase. She was all packed. 'I'm going to miss Kai and the Teys. And you.' Her heart was close to breaking with just how much she was going to miss Nick, but she summoned a smile. 'I've enjoyed our stay. It's been quite an adventure.'

'Very Lara Croft,' he said.

'I'd rather be Indiana Jones.' And when he lifted a questioning eyebrow. 'It's the hat.'

'I can see you in the hat,' he said, his eyes darkening. 'I can see you in nothing but the hat.'

'First the necklace, now the hat.' She could do this; get through this. Her brothers always told her she could banter with the best of them. 'Maybe you're developing an accessories fetish.'

'The necklace was spectacular,' he said with a wistful sigh. 'The necklace will haunt me until the day I die. Now, so will the hat. Thank you so very much.'

'Definitely an accessories fetish,' she said. 'I'm thinking shoes now. Stilettos. That might work for you too.'

'It's not the accessories.'

'It's not?'

'No.' He was close, very close. 'You're not wearing your rings.'

'They're in the bathroom. I hadn't forgotten them. I just...' Hadn't had the heart to leave them on. Hadn't been able to bear the pretence any longer. She didn't finish her sentence.

He went into the bathroom, came out with them in his hand.

'You want me to wear them,' she said, and felt her heart shatter into pieces. Of course he did. They weren't done here yet. Not quite.

'No. You don't have to wear them if you don't want to,' he said quietly. 'The thing is, I've been thinking about what I'm going to do next too. I have a plan as well.' And with a deep, ragged breath, 'I want you to keep the rings.'

'You're giving them to me?' Fine tremors racked her body as she looked away. 'You know I can't accept them.'

'I'm not giving them to you.' He put his hand on her shoulder and turned her back to face him, and now he could feel her trembling too. His eyes widened, and he stroked his hand down her arm as if to soothe her, but he didn't let her go. Instead, he captured her hand in his and traced the knuckles of her wedding finger with his thumb. 'Actually, I suppose I am giving them to you, technically speaking, but there's a catch.' His smile was crooked, his eyes uncertain. 'You have to take me too.'

'I…what?'

'I can't let you go,' he said quietly. 'I won't. So the way I figure it, you're going to have to marry me for real.'

'I…you want to marry me?'

'That's the plan,' he said. 'Of course, it does depend on you saying *yes* to the plan. And it would really help my confidence if you stopped shaking.'

'My brothers are going to kill you,' she said faintly. 'We've only known each other a week.'

'Was that a yes?'

'I'll drive you crazy.' She couldn't think straight, couldn't break free of the blossoming joy that threatened to engulf her. Nick loved her! He wanted to marry her! If anything, her trembling increased.

'Was *that* a yes?' he wanted to know. 'I'm taking that as a yes. But I'm going to need a declaration of love as well. Just to be sure.'

'You want to hear me say I love you?'

'It's a crucial part of the plan,' he said gruffly.

'I love you,' she said, bringing her hands up to frame his beautiful, beloved face, laughing when his arms came around her as if he'd never let her go. 'Yes, I'll marry you. I'm going to be the best corporate wife you've ever seen.'

'No!' He was half laughing and wholly alarmed as he picked her up in his arms and headed towards the bed. 'I don't want a corporate wife.' And with a catch in his voice that pierced her to the core, 'All I want is you.'

Jasmine, John and Kai were on hand to bid them farewell as they left for the airport the following morning. They didn't feel like business associates, these lovely, generous people, thought Hallie; they felt like family. 'Thank you,' she said warmly, holding out her hand to John. 'For your hospitality and your kindness. It was a pleasure meeting you.'

She turned to Jasmine next as Nick shook hands with John and added his thanks to hers. 'I'm going to miss you,' she said as she embraced the younger girl. 'Keep in touch.'

And then there was Kai, standing by the front door, a little apart from Jasmine and her father as he waited to drive them to the airport. 'Thanks for keeping me company yesterday. I appreciated it,' she told him with a brush of her lips to his cheek and had the satisfaction of seeing him smile, just a little. 'Still leaving for the Mainland?'

'Maybe just for a visit.'

'Maybe you should consider taking a travelling companion.'

Kai's smile grew a fraction wider. 'Take care, Hallie Cooper.'

Hallie watched as Nick completed his farewells, an affectionate hug for Jasmine and a simple heartfelt thank-you for Kai. They'd been through so much together—all five of them—that lies and half-truths no longer seemed appropriate. Had never been appropriate, thought Hallie wryly, not really. But she had no wish to upset things just as they were leaving. No wish to watch this comfortable intimacy turn to wariness and suspicion, so she kept her mouth firmly shut on the subject of her fictitious marriage to Nick and comforted herself with the knowledge that next time she saw them she *would* be married to him.

Nick joined her by the door and Hallie would have turned to leave but for Jasmine, who'd retrieved a bright red parcel from the entrance table and was holding it out towards her. 'For you and Nick,' she said impishly. 'From my father and I.'

Oh, dear. With all the excitement of the past couple of days she'd completely forgotten to get a parting gift for *them*. The corporate wife had slipped up again. 'I, ah, really wasn't expecting a parting gift,' she said awkwardly.

'Open it,' urged Jasmine.

So she opened it and stared down in astonishment at the little jade horse she'd so admired the first time she'd met John. 'Oh, my Lord,' she whispered, looking to Nick for explanation, but he looked as baffled as she was. What kind of parting gift was this? Had they gone nuts? Parting gifts were small, inexpensive mementos of a person's stay. Chopsticks were parting gifts, or a pretty silk scarf… Nothing wrong with a packet of fragrant green tea leaves either, come to think of it, but this… This was crazy. She didn't understand the gesture at all. 'I don't know what to say,' she said frankly. 'It's absolutely exquisite. But it's not a parting gift.'

'Of course not.' John Tey's mischievous smile was remarkably like his daughter's. 'It's a wedding present.'

CHAPTER TEN

FLIGHT 128 from Hong Kong to Heathrow touched down with a screech and a swerve at five p.m. on a grey and blustery afternoon, but neither the weather nor the bumpy landing could dim Hallie's happiness. She was manicured, pedicured, pampered and polished and was corporate wife chic in her lightweight camel-coloured trousers and pink camisole and jacket. Her shoes matched her top, her handbag was Hermès, and Nick was at her side. She was the woman who had it all and it was all she'd ever dreamed of.

That didn't mean she was a pushover.

'I still can't believe you didn't tell me you told John we weren't married,' she said as she stared down at the little jade horse in her handbag. What with that and the funeral vase, customs was going to be a real treat.

'I was going to tell you,' said Nick. 'Right after I proposed and you accepted, but I figured I'd leave it a few minutes on account of the timing not being quite right. I wanted you to be quite sure I was proposing because I wanted to and not because I'd just blown our cover.'

Ah. It was slightly disconcerting just how well Nick knew her.

'Then, when I was just about to tell you, I got distracted.'

'By what?'

'You don't remember?' He sighed heavily but his eyes gleamed with lazy satisfaction. 'How soon a wife forgets.'

Hallie did remember. And blushed at the memory of their fiery lovemaking. 'After *that.*'

'After that my brain had turned to mush,' said Nick and it was Hallie's turn to sigh. It was almost impossible to stay angry with Nick when he was being charming, which was most of the time, but she didn't want to set a precedent.

'We're partners,' she said firmly. 'I expect you to share these little details with me.'

'Ah.' It was a very uncomfortable sounding 'Ah'. 'There's something else I should probably mention before we go through customs and out into the arrivals terminal,' said Nick.

She stopped, mid-stride, and eyed him narrowly. Nick's mouth twitched as he pulled her into his arms and his mouth descended on hers, regardless of the people streaming past them. By the time the kiss ended, she was dazed, aroused and doubtless dishevelled, but she wasn't distracted. 'You were saying?' she said smoothly.

'Clea's meeting us here.'

'So?' To Hallie's way of thinking that was hardly a problem. 'I like your mother.'

'So do I,' said Nick. 'It's just one of those details I

thought might be worth sharing.' Then they tackled customs and stepped through the final set of doors and out into the arrivals area.

'There she is,' said Nick, and there she was, a vision splendid in magenta and lime chiffon with a leopard-print handbag that matched her shoes.

'I knew it!' said Clea when they reached her. 'I knew you'd be perfect together. Mothers can sense these things.'

Hallie snickered as Nick suffered his mother's enthusiastic embrace and then she too found herself enveloped in a fragrant cloud of Clea.

'You *are* going to marry him, aren't you, dear? Let me look at you. There, of course you are!'

'Did you tell her?' muttered Nick. 'I didn't tell her.'

'Apparently mothers can sense these things,' said Hallie.

'Wait until you have children of your own. You'll see,' said Clea. 'Oh, you're going to give me such beautiful grandchildren!'

But Hallie didn't appear to be listening. She was looking past Clea, her startled gaze fixed on a dark-haired man leaning against a column some distance away. He was big and lean and all muscle, his hair was shaggy, and he was looking their way, his focus absolute. Nick watched with fatalistic calm as the man dislodged himself from the column to stand and glare at him with amber eyes as fierce and untamed as a mountain cat.

'I think you're about to meet Tristan,' said Hallie.

He'd figured as much. 'He looks a mite put out. Did you leave him a note?'

'Right there beneath the toaster. I swear.'

'I see.'

Tristan had finished taking his measure and was now staring at the hastily re-wrapped funeral vase tucked beneath Nick's arm, his expression grim.

'He knows about the vase,' she muttered.

'That's Interpol for you.'

'You're not taking this seriously enough, Nick.'

'Trust me, I am.'

From what Hallie had told him, her brothers were protective of her. And regardless of him wanting to marry her *now*, there was no denying he'd carted her off to Hong Kong under false pretences, had his wicked way with her, and allowed her to waltz, practically unprotected, into the lair of the local warlord.

Tristan started towards them.

'You're going to run, aren't you?' said Hallie morosely. 'They always run.'

'Absolutely not,' he said, tearing his gaze away from her brother to send her a reassuring smile, and then Tristan reached them, nodding politely enough to Clea before shooting his sister a wrathful, baffled glare that Nick could identify with. Then it was his turn to meet that flat, golden gaze.

'So…' Tristan let the word trail off ominously. 'How was the trip?'

'Stop that!' Hallie stepped forward to stand protectively in front of him, hands on her hips, eyes flashing. 'You be nice to him!'

Tris's gaze cut to his sister, to the wedding rings

already on her finger, and Nick saw a familiar wilful-
ness there along with no small measure of love. 'Why?'

'Because he's mine, that's why! Because I love him
and I'm going to marry him and we're going to have
beautiful babies together, so back off!'

'Babies?' echoed Tristan.

'Gorgeous, adorable babies,' said Clea, throwing in
a grandmotherly smile for good measure. 'Soon.'

'How soon?' Tristan's searing gaze cut to Clea.
Nick rolled his eyes in disbelief.

'Not that soon,' he said firmly. 'Later.' He reached out
to pull Hallie back until she was once more standing by
his side. 'Please,' he said dryly, 'don't try to help me.'

'But—'

'No.' He silenced any further protest with a warning
glance. 'I let you call the shots in Hong Kong, but you
don't have to rush to my defence here. I don't need
your protection,' he said softly. 'I don't *want* your protection. Not this time. You of all people should understand that.'

'Fine.' She sent him a glance that held equal measures of self-mockery and frustration. 'He's all yours.'

'Hard, isn't it?' Nick leaned down and kissed the
generous pout of her mouth because he couldn't resist.
'Have a little faith. Maybe we'll bond.'

'Tris doesn't bond all that well,' said Hallie, shooting her brother a dark glance.

'Don't push him, Hallie. Your brother loves you. He
only wants what's best for you.'

'That would be you,' she said with quiet certainty.

Nick looked down into Hallie's vibrant, beloved face, a smile on his lips and in his heart. 'Hold that thought,' he said. And kissed her again.

Chosen by him for business,
taken by him for pleasure…
A classic collection of office romances from
Harlequin Presents, by your favorite authors.

Coming in September:

THE BRAZILIAN BOSS'S
INNOCENT MISTRESS
by Sarah Morgan

Innocent Grace Thacker has ten minutes to persuade
ruthless Brazilian Rafael Cordeiro to help her.
Ten minutes to decide whether to leave and lose—
or settle her debts in his bed!

Also from this miniseries, coming in October:

THE BOSS'S WIFE
FOR A WEEK
by Anne McAllister

BILLIONAIRES' BRIDES

Pregnant by their princes...

Take three incredibly wealthy European princes
and match them with three beautiful, spirited women.
Add large helpings of intense emotion and passionate
attraction. Result: three unexpected pregnancies—and
three possible princesses—if those princes have their way....

Coming in September:

THE GREEK PRINCE'S CHOSEN WIFE
by Sandra Marton

Ivy Madison is pregnant with Prince Damian's baby—
as a surrogate mother! Now Damian won't let Ivy go—after
all, he didn't have the pleasure of taking her to bed before....

Available in August:

THE ITALIAN PRINCE'S PREGNANT BRIDE

Coming in October:

THE SPANISH PRINCE'S VIRGIN BRIDE

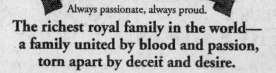

REQUEST YOUR FREE BOOKS!

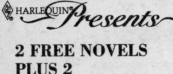

2 FREE NOVELS
PLUS 2
FREE GIFTS!

PASSION
GUARANTEED
SEDUCTION

YES! Please send me 2 FREE Harlequin Presents® novels and my 2 FREE gifts. After receiving them, if I don't wish to receive any more books, I can return the shipping statement marked "cancel." If I don't cancel, I will receive 6 brand-new novels every month and be billed just $3.80 per book in the U.S., or $4.47 per book in Canada, plus 25¢ shipping and handling per book and applicable taxes, if any*. That's a savings of close to 15% off the cover price! I understand that accepting the 2 free books and gifts places me under no obligation to buy anything. I can always return a shipment and cancel at any time. Even if I never buy another book from Harlequin, the two free books and gifts are mine to keep forever.

106 HDN EEXK   306 HDN EEXV

Name _____ (PLEASE PRINT)

Address _____ Apt. #

City _____ State/Prov. _____ Zip/Postal Code

Signature (if under 18, a parent or guardian must sign)

Mail to the **Harlequin Reader Service®:**
IN U.S.A.: P.O. Box 1867, Buffalo, NY 14240-1867
IN CANADA: P.O. Box 609, Fort Erie, Ontario L2A 5X3

Not valid to current Harlequin Presents subscribers.

Want to try two free books from another line?
Call 1-800-873-8635 or visit www.morefreebooks.com.

* Terms and prices subject to change without notice. NY residents add applicable sales tax. Canadian residents will be charged applicable provincial taxes and GST. This offer is limited to one order per household. All orders subject to approval. Credit or debit balances in a customer's account(s) may be offset by any other outstanding balance owed by or to the customer. Please allow 4 to 6 weeks for delivery.

Your Privacy: Harlequin is committed to protecting your privacy. Our Privacy Policy is available online at www.eHarlequin.com or upon request from the Reader Service. From time to time we make our lists of customers available to reputable firms who may have a product or service of interest to you. If you would prefer we not share your name and address, please check here. ☐

HP07